## "I haven't to[l]

### my seven ex-

"Seven?" Grady's [...] plopped down onto the sofa beside Hilary with a dazed look on his face.

She nodded glumly. "Grady, a practical man like you needs order in his life, not some flake that goes flying off at two-thirty in the morning to bail out a friend from jail."

He shook his head as though to clear it. "Why don't you let me be the judge of that?"

She groaned wearily. "That's exactly what the fiancés said. And I made them all miserable and crazy."

Grady's face took on a determined expression that Hilary had never seen before. "None of that matters."

"It *does* matter, Grady!" She had to convince him. "Go find some nice sensible woman with a station wagon and support hose...."

Grady grasped her arms and gazed into her eyes. "I don't want a sensible woman, dammit! Hilary, I want you!"

This book is **Sheryl Danson**'s first Temptation novel. Originally a fan of historical romances, she had overlooked contemporary series romances because she thought "they didn't have sex in those books!" A girlfriend set her straight by giving her a shopping bag full of them to read. Lucky for us, they piqued Sheryl's interest and inspired her to write *Always a Fiancée*. Her sexy, humorous style was so impressive, we just had to snatch it up for our readers! She currently lives in Pennsylvania with her husband. Welcome to Temptation, Sheryl!

# ALWAYS A FIANCÉE

**SHERYL DANSON**

*Harlequin Books*

TORONTO • NEW YORK • LONDON
AMSTERDAM • PARIS • SYDNEY • HAMBURG
STOCKHOLM • ATHENS • TOKYO • MILAN
MADRID • WARSAW • BUDAPEST • AUCKLAND

To Gary with love,
for being the only man in town who doesn't
have to identify himself to 911

Published March 1993

ISBN 0-373-25534-9

ALWAYS A FIANCÉE

# 1

IT ALL BEGAN WITH A CRASH—three simultaneous crashes, actually—and the horrible sound of grinding steel. There were no squealing tires, no blaring horns, no screams warning of imminent disaster. It happened so fast, no one had a chance to anticipate it. No one, of course, including the man with his dark head slumped over the steering wheel of his Thunderbird hardtop. He was not in pain or unconscious, but outraged by the sheer senselessness of the accident that had left his vintage car embracing a lamppost in row five of the Giant Eagle Supermarket parking lot.

"Damn!" Grady Thompson swore, his fingers tightening on the wheel. It was probably all that was left intact of the automobile that had embodied his oldest, fondest dreams. His obsession with the 1964 T-Bird dated back to the year the model was new—six long years before he'd even learned to drive. He'd vowed then that one day he'd have one, though at the time he'd had no idea what owning the car would entail. A classic T-Bird wasn't simply a means of transportation; it was the investment of a lifetime.

He'd paid several times Ford's original sticker price, and that had been only the beginning. Every inch of the automobile had been lovingly restored, at considerable time and expense. The insurance was positively extortionary. There was also the cost of maintaining his other car, The Clunker, which was twenty-five years and twenty-five thousand miles newer and served as his primary vehicle. It ventured out in the snow and rain and salt while the T-Bird sat safely inside its garage. He'd been so careful to protect it from the elements and bad neighborhoods and careless drivers, but had never considered that he could wind up being his car's worst enemy. In the end, he had been the one who had done it in—and simply by smacking it into a stationary object.

Though he didn't want to do it, he raised his head and peered over the dash for a preliminary appraisal of the damage. The grille, bumper, hood, and one fender were all going to need extensive work, and those were merely the most evident of the casualties. He was sure that once he took a good look at it, there was going to be more. Much more.

Cursing at that thought, he got out of the car and slammed the door behind him. After glancing at the two other collisions that had been coincidental with his and muttering his sincere—albeit irrational—relief that he hadn't been alone in his idiocy, he marched over to the red Mazda hatchback in row six and brusquely ordered its occupant, "Don't go anywhere! I want to talk to you when I'm finished!" Without waiting for an answer, he spun on his heel and stalked away from the woman.

Hilary Campbell gaped after him as he crossed the parking lot. While she knew the observation was pretty much pointless—not just because he had the disposition of a wounded grizzly bear, but also because she'd sworn off the male of the species (human, not bear) for good this time—she couldn't help noticing that he had nice buns. Very nice, in fact.

He didn't *look* like the kind of man who was in a perpetual snit with the world. If anything, he'd seemed astounded by his own outburst. But what on earth had set him off at *her*? She hadn't done anything—not that she remembered, anyway—unless maybe she'd bumped into his cart with hers, breaking his eggs in the process? Though she hadn't noticed any sign of injury before he'd gone stomping off (to commiserate with his fellow kamikazes), she wondered if his crankiness might be the result of thumping his head during the car wreck. She hadn't seen it, but she'd heard it quite clearly. The evidence of it was now strewn from one end of the parking lot to the other like the aftermath of an air raid.

Equally compelling, and far more interesting, was the proof that her initial assessment had been right on the money. That tush gave his jeans a reason for living, and the shoulders above were as broad and solid as his tush was tight and firm. Acting on impulse, without taking time to think it through, muster some restraint, and repress the notion, she sent a piercing wolf whistle flying through the air after him. That it found its mark—and neither amused nor pleased him—was confirmed by the killing look he shot back at her a second later. Undaunted by the tacit reproach in that glare, she flashed him a saucy grin that only seemed to aggravate him further.

In truth, that was precisely what it did.

Grumbling a few choice words about the relative intelligence level of a woman who could wreak this much havoc without batting an eyelash, he made his way toward the head-on collision. While both drivers involved in *that* crash were shaken, angry and embarrassed—emotions he understood entirely too well—the good news was that neither had been injured. "I'm a police officer," he assured them with a professional demeanor that owed more to his sense of responsibility than reality. "We're gonna have to file a report on this. Let me check on the other guy, and then I'll be back to take statements from both of you."

As he walked away from the two men, Grady glanced around, looking for the woman who belonged to the little red Mazda. Though she seemed to have vanished into thin air, the Mazda itself was still parked in row six. He hoped the fact that she was on foot meant she hadn't gone far and intended to return sometime soon.

The second accident was worse than the first—but then, he'd known it would be. This driver had hit three parked cars before finally coming to a halt. After verifying that no one had been hurt, he took statements from everyone involved, called for tow trucks, and located and placated the owners of the parked cars. They were every bit as irate as Grady had expected them to be, particularly when neither he nor the driver who had hit them would explain what had caused the accident. He didn't cite any of the drivers for the collisions, because he couldn't bring himself to do it. God knew he was just as guilty as they were.

Once all the drivers and smashed vehicles were on their way and the peace maintained (more or less), he walked back to his own car and saw that the cause of the accidents had returned to the scene of the crime.

She was perched on the crumpled hood of the T-Bird, one pink-suede-thonged foot propped on the mangled bumper while the other dangled from her crossed leg, its shoe slapping restlessly against her sole. His gaze raked up shapely bare legs to the hem of an indecently short Calvin Klein jean miniskirt made even more so by her present position. Above that was a strip of bare midriff topped by an abbreviated pink tank top that was scarcely more than a bra, and revealed more than it hid of her generously rounded breasts. He dragged his eyes up to her face, which was more than worthy of being attached to that body. Her complexion was like gleaming opal, palest white with touches of fiery pink, and her features were as fine and delicate. A pile of hair, somewhere between blond and brown, tumbled around her shoulders. Dominating her face were the brightest blue eyes he'd ever seen.

Grady knew he'd looked too long, but he didn't care. From the looks of his car, he was already going to pay for it through the nose. He might as well get his money's worth.

"See anything you like?"

It wasn't an invitation. Instead, she sounded peevish, like a passerby who had seen the whole thing but didn't want to get involved and wished she'd had the foresight to bolt before anyone realized she was a potential witness. Didn't she know that her role in the fiasco far exceeded that of innocent bystander? That she'd been single-handedly responsible for all those wrecked cars? That she was heaping gross insult on top of grievous injury by *sitting* on his? If anyone had a right to be peevish, it certainly wasn't her. "What are you doing up there?" he demanded.

"Waiting. Just like you told me to." She shrugged.

While Grady didn't think either nuance was deliberate, that motion of her shoulders managed to be provoking and provocative at the same time—and his reactions to it proved to be just as contradictory. First—and not surprisingly—he felt a strong jolt of indignant disbelief at her nonchalant attitude toward a calamity everyone else knew she'd precipitated. Accompanying that, however, was a rush of the most acute masculine awareness he'd felt in longer than he could remember, one that was, under the circumstances, so utterly unwanted and unexpected, it nettled him even further. "Get off there," he snapped irritably. "And where did you go, before?"

"I went to get cigarettes. I'm back." Underscoring the claim and, coincidentally, the unsettling effect she had on his faculties, she hopped off the hood of the car, her skirt riding up even higher. As she dropped the cigarette and ground it out under the toe of one pink sandal, he couldn't help noticing that her toenails were polished to match. "So, what do you want with me? I didn't see any of the accidents."

"No kidding. What were you doing?"

"I was taking off my sweater."

"Exactly." It was at the precise moment when she'd pulled the sweater over her head, revealing what had appeared to be a nude torso underneath, that all hell had broken loose.

"Exactly?" Hilary echoed skeptically. It was quite simple, actually, or at least she thought it ought to be. She'd put on the sweater before going into the air-conditioned chill of the supermarket, and then taken it off again once she'd come back out into the eighty-degree heat—unseasonable for April in Pittsburgh but there nonetheless. "Is there a law against that?"

"Come on." He stalked around to the passenger side of the wrecked T-Bird, and she automatically followed as far as the biggest pleat in the fender. "You're coming with me."

At that announcement, she balked, eyeing him cagily as she asked, "You want to think about that one some more?"

He yanked open the car door and frowned at her. "Get in."

If there was one thing Hilary knew when she saw it, it was the distinctive look of a normally sane, self-restrained man who was having the limits of both attributes put to the ultimate test by circumstances beyond his (and her) control.

It didn't particularly worry her; experience with the phenomenon had taught her that all she had to do was wait until it was over.

In the meantime, she told him patiently but firmly, "I'm not going anywhere with you."

"I'd say you don't have a whole hell of a lot of choice in the matter," he muttered disgruntledly. "You're under arrest."

"What?" *Arrest* wasn't usually part of the scenario. In fact, it never had been before.

"You heard me—get in there." He jabbed his finger into the opening, emphasizing his command.

In her moment of shocked reaction, she actually did as he ordered. After shutting the door, he strode around to the other side of the car and slid behind the wheel. "We'll have to take your car, though. This one's not going anywhere until the wrecker comes back to haul it away."

"I'm not going anywhere with you," Hilary repeated, as if saying it again would make it a fact. As she recovered from the initial impact of the word *arrest* and realized she'd gotten into his car under her own steam, she twisted around in the seat, going for the door handle—and freedom.

Before she could open the door, he caught her by the elbow, holding it firmly as he reached for the microphone of the police radio with his other, free hand. "You want to think about that one some more?" he asked. "Stay put until I get through here."

She stayed, having no viable alternative. While his grip wasn't tight enough to hurt, it was as secure as a vise—as she discovered when her attempt to extricate her arm only succeeded in grinding the back of his hand into her breast. Covered as it was by a single layer of thin, pink cotton, she could feel each of his hard knuckles press into her soft flesh. She guessed he did, too, because he paused momentarily in his discussion with the dispatcher to turn his head and frown at her as if she'd done it on purpose.

"Come on, let's go," he said as soon as he signed off. When he released her to disconnect the radio, she thought again about making a run for it, but rejected the idea—which didn't mean she intended to go along docilely.

"I told you already. I'm not going anywhere with you." She crossed her arms over her chest and wriggled her bottom into the seat, figuring the wrecker could just haul her away with the car.

Exasperation apparent on his face, he got out of the car, locked the radio in the trunk, and circled to the passenger door. Opening it, he extended his hand to her.

"No."

"Get out of the car."

"Are you crazy?"

"I wasn't crazy until twenty minutes ago." He looked as if he was telling the truth, verifying her earlier speculation that he was ordinarily the most reasonable of men. At the moment, however, reason was still on vacation. His hand closed over her forearm, his fingers circling it and overlapping. "You have the right to remain silent . . ."

As much as she hadn't wanted to get into the car earlier, she most definitely didn't want to get out now. She planted both feet on the floorboards and stared up at him. "What are you doing?"

"Arresting you." He continued Mirandizing her and gave her wrist a little tug, trying to persuade her to get out.

Hilary ignored the suggestion, though the reiteration of the word *arrest* was more than she could dismiss. "I know that. I watch television. What I don't understand is *why.*"

"Attractive nuisance."

"I thought that was a swimming pool without a fence," she pointed out.

"It's also a half-naked woman in a parking lot," he barked. "Do you realize that you wrecked seven cars?"

"I didn't do anything! My car wasn't even involved! It wasn't even running! I wasn't even in it!" She braced herself against the inside of the doorframe and held on.

"Last chance to go peaceably!"

"What're you gonna do? Shoot me?"

"Resisting arrest! Let go, dammit!" he added as he bent down, seized her around the waist, and swung her up and over his shoulder in a fireman's carry. She noted, fleetingly and irrelevantly, that he felt every bit as solid as he looked. While her altered perspective might have confirmed the corollary that his buns were spectacular, she didn't have leisure time to look.

"Put me down!" Hilary insisted, wriggling. She thumped her fist against his back, just once to get his attention. Tired and hungry, she wanted to get home before her ice cream turned into soup.

"Assaulting a police officer..." Grady swatted her rear, just hard enough to startle her into cooperation. He was overdue at work, his T-Bird was wrecked, and he didn't have time for this.

She squawked angrily. She was entitled. Instead of denim, his hand landed against warm, smooth skin and something silky. He winced as his eyes skittered sideways to verify his suspicion. Yep, shiny pink nylon. He blushed and reached to tug the hem of the skirt so it would cover her now-exposed behind. His hand closed to grip the hem of the skirt and grabbed something else altogether.

Her yowl of indignation was even louder and more justified this time, and Grady tried to retrieve his hand. He really did. If only she hadn't reacted to the intrusion by clamping her thighs together, trapping his hand between them. He hoped he could get it out of there before she drew blood where her fingernails were digging into the center of his back.

By accident or design, her knee made contact with his solar plexus, knocking the wind out of him. Unable to hold her and breathe at the same time, he let her tumble to the ground, where she sprawled out on the pavement with all the dignity of an abandoned Barbie doll. Her skirt had worked its way up to her hips. Her top was rolled up, confirming his hunch that she wore nothing but bare skin beneath the scandalous piece of stretchy stuff. Blushing hotly, he held his hands up, palms out, in a gesture denying culpability, and then turned away to allow her relative privacy to pull herself together.

Turning his back on her might have been the decent thing to do, but it hadn't been a particularly bright move, Grady realized an instant later as something rigid struck his back just above the spot where she'd tried to impale him with her nails. Whatever it was, it hurt, even with the protection of his leather shoulder holster and the jacket he wore to cover it. When he turned around to face her, he saw it was her shoe—that blasted pink thong. She seemed to have developed a whole new defense based on the use of the shoe—and she was good at it.

She backed away from him, blue eyes flashing defiantly, daring him to tell her she was still under arrest. He couldn't do it. He couldn't speak. He was too occupied with staring at her heaving breasts as they pressed against the soft stretchy cotton, their nipples erect and jutting out. Absurdly, his body reacted to the sight. He felt the strained fly of his jeans and prayed she didn't notice.

She did. Pointing at him, she stridently accused, "You pervert!"

The worst part was, he felt like one. Under any reasonable circumstance, such scorn would have been withering. His body, however, refused to acknowledge that basic principle.

"I'm calling a cop!" she threatened.

"I *am* a cop!"

"I'm calling *another* cop!"

"You can't do that! You're still under arrest!"

"Why? Because a sex-starved, adolescent pervert was so busy gawking, he wrecked his car?"

"Get in the car!" Grady ground out through teeth that were as tightly compressed as the region beneath the fly of his jeans. The pressure in that vicinity had surpassed painful and become simply excruciating.

Hilary got into the car, not because he'd ordered her to do it, but because she didn't intend to spend the rest of her life in a parking-lot standoff with a lunatic pervert who happened to have great buns. Several moments later, she heard a knock on the passenger window and turned her head toward the sound.

Never had she regretted having a small car as much as she did at that instant. The fly of his jeans was at eye level outside the passenger window, the obvious indication of his arousal still straining against the denim. Groaning, she closed her eyes and dropped her head against the steering wheel, trying to stop the funny little pain in her chest.

"Are you gonna unlock the door or am I supposed to lash myself to the roof?" The voice sounded closer. It was. The crotch had moved around the car to stand outside the open window on the driver's side, inches away from her.

"Why don't you lie down behind the car, and I'll run you over?" she suggested dryly.

"Is that any way to talk to an officer of the law?"

"How do I know you even *are* a cop?"

Grady shoved his hand into his back pocket, pulling the already-taut denim even tighter across the front. It wasn't helping that all that he could see from his vantage point were the full breasts in the skimpy top and the dark shadow of her thighs. He pulled out the wallet and a small, embarrassingly distinctive foil packet fell out and fluttered to the ground. He kicked it under the car, hoping she hadn't seen it.

She had. A small sound somewhere between a giggle and a choke issued from within the car.

He opened the wallet to show her his badge, just as he had done a thousand times before. Unlike the other thousand times, another foil packet, just like the first, dropped from it into her lap.

A delicate hand emerged from the window, the offensive object lying in its palm. "Yours, I believe?"

Grady grabbed the damn thing and shoved it into the front pocket of his jeans, out of sight, as quickly as possible.

"Keep all your shields together?"

He groaned, slamming his forehead down against the roof of the car. He wished she hadn't said that.

Hilary wished she hadn't said it, too. As he lowered his head to the car roof, he'd moved closer to the car so quickly that she didn't have a chance to pull her hand back inside the window. He ran into it. She hoped he hadn't noticed it.

His groan of utter mortification told her that he had. He dropped to an uneasy crouch and braced his head against the center support of the car. After taking a deep breath, he asked, "If I lie down behind the car, do you *promise* to run me over?"

"This is a small car," she pointed out matter-of-factly. "I don't think it would kill you, just do painful damage."

"It doesn't matter." He looked up at her pitifully. "Can we start over? I'm Grady Thompson."

It was a considerable relief to have his face, instead of his fly, next to her car window. It was a nice face: soft brown eyes, an unruly tangle of dark brown hair, strong features—straight nose, square jaw, and full, sensuous lips.

*Stop that!* she told herself sharply. *Remember that you've sworn off men. Remember why.* "Hilary Campbell," she forced out.

"Are you absolutely positive you don't want to run me over?"

"That all depends. Am I still under arrest?"

"Are you kidding? Do you think I want to tell this story in front of a judge?"

She considered the question and then shook her head.

"I know I'm not exactly in a position to ask favors, but I'd really appreciate it if you could give me a ride to the station."

Chewing at her bottom lip, Hilary deliberated the request for a moment, then nodded. What harm could there be in that? A couple of minutes, and then she'd be rid of him. "Sure." She leaned across the gearshift to unlock the passenger door. "Get in."

Grady was still on the driver's side because he'd been watching the way her skirt rode up at the back when she reached for the lock. "Oh . . . Okay. Thanks."

He circled the car, opened the door, and stared down at the passenger seat, which was already occupied. Very occupied. "What should I do with this stuff?" It was a pile of books, an umbrella, a purse as big as a suitcase, and a stretched canvas—forty-eight by forty-eight and blank. "You paint?"

"No, my roommate does. Just throw it all in the back."

"You've got to be kidding. Where?" The back seat and hatchback both looked full to him. There were piles of books, magazines and newspapers, cups and bags from every fast-food place in North America, a pair of street skates, several shoes, possibly with mates, one mitten and a couple of cans of motor oil. Inexplicably draped over the whole mess was a stunner of a shimmery black cocktail dress. "Is Jimmy Hoffa back there?"

Hilary stopped pitching items from the passenger seat into the back and gave him a baleful look. "Want to take it all out and search?"

"Not on your life. But I may have to arrest you, after all."

"For what?"

"Hauling trash without a license."

"Do you want a ride or not?"

"I'll behave."

"What *is* this fixation you have with arresting me? Are you the domineering type or something?"

"Got me." He shrugged and carefully eased himself into the front seat. "You might have to keep me. I think I'm stuck."

"Why don't you move the seat back?" She reached for the handle behind his calves and he pulled his legs out of the way.

"That's okay. I'll do it." Grady was finally getting himself under control, and he suspected that if she touched him, even accidentally, all his good intentions would go flying right out the window. "That's better. Sort of."

The ride to the precinct did nothing to soothe Grady's already-frayed nerves. Treating the speed limits with the most cavalier disregard he'd ever witnessed, Hilary zipped through the narrow, winding, potholed streets indigenous to Pittsburgh, ran three yellow lights in as many blocks, and never shifted below second gear at stop signs. Meanwhile, she passed a cigarette from one hand to the other more than she actually smoked it, tucked a soda cup between her knees when she needed a free hand to shift, sang intermittent spurts of whatever was playing on the radio, and carried on two remarkably lucid conversations—one with him and one with other drivers. In spite of the state of his nerves, he found the entire spectacle appealing.

Deep down inside, Grady knew it wasn't her driving that made him nervous. It was the short skirt and bare thighs with the McDonald's cup held firmly and unselfconsciously between them. It was the scanty top against which her nipples were so clearly defined. And it was the sensual way her lips moved when she sang.

He wasn't aware that he was staring until she caught him in the act. At the time, she was fastening her hair back into a clip during a red light at which she had deigned to stop. She had dug it, one-handed, out of the compartment between the two seats while she was driving.

"Is something wrong?" She looked genuinely puzzled, though he knew that surely someone, somewhere along the way, must have mentioned to her that driving a car was supposed to command her full attention.

"Don't you find it distracting to do all these other things while you're driving?" he asked tactfully.

She shrugged again, a gesture he was becoming attached to with a speed that was nearly as alarming as Hilary's driving. In addition to being adorable, it made all the interesting parts of her body move in intriguing ways. "I don't know. I always have. Maybe it's my short attention span. Maybe it's because I don't have enough time to get to everything unless I do it all at once.

"Damn you, anyway, if you're going, get going!"

Grady flinched before he realized that she was addressing another driver.

Before he could recover from her outburst, she spoke again, her voice returning to its former soft timbre. "Hold this, will you?" It was the soda. When she used her fingers to rub away the damp places it had left on her thighs, Grady told himself to look away, but he couldn't stop watching her. "It was getting cold," she explained guilelessly, and he ordered himself to pull it together with a stern reminder that he was closer to forty than fourteen. He wondered how old she was.

She turned up the car radio to a level he feared might shatter the windows like a Memorex commercial. It was playing The Doors' "Touch Me" and she sang along in a deeply husky voice that, while out of proportion with her diminutive size, was startlingly seductive. At the realization that she knew all the words to the old song, as she had to several others, he decided she must be older than she appeared.

He reached out and turned the radio down several decibels. "How old are you?"

"Twenty-six."

"Really?"

"Really. That's all right," she consoled him. "The man at the liquor store doesn't believe me, either." She reached down and turned the radio back up again, effectively putting an end to his attempt at conversation.

*Twenty-six*, Grady marveled. He never would have guessed it. He'd thought she was about nineteen, and entirely too young for him—a conclusion he'd reached based on her tiny size, her trendy clothing, and the fact that she hadn't seemed to notice that the song she was singing was as blatantly erotic as only Jim Morrison could be.

Mid-chorus, that last thought occurred to Hilary, too, and she wondered if it would be too conspicuous if she changed the station, turned the radio off altogether, or simply pushed Grady Thompson out the door. She needed another disaster like she needed a hole in the head, and the questions he was asking seemed to indicate he was interested in her in ways that had nothing to do with seven wrecked cars. If that wasn't a disaster in the making, she didn't know what was.

Since the car had started moving, she'd done her best to treat him in a casual manner she'd hoped would discourage his unhealthy interest, but it didn't seem to be getting through to him. God, he was thickheaded. It was probably that he wasn't used to rejection. A man who looked like him probably didn't encounter it very often. The wavy brown hair that seemed to thwart all attempts at control, the glimmering spaniel-brown eyes, the strong, large-boned features that set off the surprisingly soft curve of his mouth . . . Her own mouth went dry at the image, and she reached out with her hand in a silent plea for the return of her drink.

When he didn't respond, she tapped his shoulder. It was as broad and solid as she remembered.

"Drink?" she forced herself to ask casually, if loudly to compete with the sound of the radio.

"What?" He turned the radio back down again.

"May I have my drink, please?"

Holding it by the top, he placed it in her hand without touching her.

"Thanks." Hilary took a sip and put the drink between her knees again.

"Hilary, can I call you?"

His voice had a touch of hesitation in it that Hilary found enormously appealing. With effort, she suppressed her response. "I don't think so," she answered at last.

"Look, I know I acted like a jerk—"

"It's not that...."

"I'm really not a pervert—"

"I'm aware of that. You've been on your best behavior since you got in the car."

"You've got a husband, a fiancé, a . . . ?"

"No."

"Then why?"

"It's not a good idea," she said firmly.

"What?"

"It's not—"

"I heard that. I just don't understand it."

Pulling to a stop in the no-parking zone in front of the station, Hilary shifted into neutral, but didn't put on the brake or turn off the engine. Either action seemed entirely too long-term, when she was only stopping long enough to get rid of him. "It seems plain enough to me."

Grady pulled up on the brake handle and reached for the ignition.

"No," she insisted.

He turned the key, cutting off the motor. "What does that mean?"

"No? Negative. Uh-uh. Wrong bus stop, bucko—"

"Don't be cute."

"I can't help it." She thought that was her whole problem, actually.

"You must have time for a movie—"

"No."

"Dinner?"

"No." She rolled her eyes heavenward, pleading for divine intervention. A bolt of lightning would do. "Look, I can't get involved with anyone. It's not you."

"A drink?"

"You're not listening, are you?"

"Of course not. It's ridiculous."

"It is not. It's the truth."

"You can't avoid me, you know."

"Want to make a bet? You don't know where I live, my phone number . . ."

"I have your license number." He didn't, but he'd get it off her plate when she drove away.

"Damn." She hadn't thought of that. The determination his statement implied stiffened her resolve, which had started to crumble in the face of her undeniable attraction to him. As added reinforcement, she mentally listed seven good reasons why agreeing to go out with Grady Thompson was not a good idea.

Grady reached for the door handle and it came off in his hand. "I guess you're stuck with me now."

"Wrong again. The pin just fell out. It does that all the time." Silently, she cursed her indifferent maintenance on the car and wished she'd listened to her father more often when he'd lectured her about such things.

"Maybe I should just pitch it into the Bermuda Triangle." He indicated the back seat. "We'll never find it there."

"Don't even think it," she warned.

"I'll let you fix the door and get rid of me if you let me kiss you." Grady didn't know what possessed him to say that, but then, he didn't really know what had possessed him since the moment he'd first set eyes on her. He kept acting like someone he didn't even know—or *want* to know, for that matter.

"I think you've done quite enough groping for one day," she said sharply. "Besides, all you have to do is reach out the window and you can open the door with the handle outside."

"That's no fun."

"Out. Now."

She looked so indignant that Grady didn't press the issue. The remark about groping suggested she still might think he was a pervert. After dropping the handle in the compartment between the seats, he reached out the window to open the door. Once outside, he circled the car to the driver's side and crouched next to the window. "Bye. Thanks for the ride."

"You're welcome. And I am sorry about your car."

Grady shook his head sadly. "Don't worry about it. I'm sure they can fix it."

Hilary started the car again and let off the brake.

"I'll call you."

"You will not." She released the clutch and started away at a clip that implied she couldn't get away fast enough.

"I will! And you *will* go out with me!" Grady wasn't sure whether or not she'd heard him.

The Mazda came to an abrupt halt and her head craned back through the open window. Clearly she had. "I will not!"

"Yes, you will!"

# 2

BECAUSE HILARY still had it in second gear, the little red Mazda protested loudly when she forced it to take off again. Grady had plenty of time to get the license number, which he immediately noted in the small spiral-bound notepad he always carried. He scrawled Hilary's name above, though chances were slim to none he'd ever forget to whom CAUTION belonged. A familiar voice from behind let him know there had been at least one witness to his latest spate of aberrant behavior.

"Thompson, is that you?" Grady's partner, Charlie Landis, sounded as if he suspected it was an alien that only looked like Grady Thompson. "Since when have you taken to screaming at blondes in little red cars?"

"Since this afternoon," Grady muttered, consoling himself with the knowledge that Charlie was alone and hadn't been around to see his earlier performance. Otherwise, he'd *never* have heard the last of it.

"It's not like you," Charlie said, sounding amazed. As he'd observed a couple of hundred times since they'd first met as rookies fifteen years earlier, Grady was ordinarily as quiet and sensible as his grandmother's crepe-soled shoes.

"I know," he said glumly.

"Where's your car?"

"Wrecked."

"The T-Bird is wrecked?" Charlie's voice rose at least two octaves. "What happened?"

Grady pointed vaguely in the direction the Mazda had gone.

"She didn't hit you. There wasn't a scratch on her car."

"I ran it into a lamppost," he answered glumly.

Charlie wrinkled his forehead in confusion and then started to chuckle. While the Mazda itself may not have touched Grady's car, the blonde inside certainly seemed to have struck a live nerve or two in Grady.

"It's not funny," Grady said indignantly.

"Not in the least." Charlie couldn't stop laughing. "Where are the doughnuts?"

"I didn't get them. And I don't want to talk about it anymore." Grady stalked into the station, and Charlie, still laughing, trailed along after him. He was still chuckling with amusement when Grady ripped the page from its spiral moorings with a great deal more vigor than the task required, slapped it onto the counter with an announcement that he wanted an address and telephone number as soon as possible, and continued into their office.

Confounded into speechlessness by the detective's atypically gruff behavior, the clerk behind the counter looked to Charlie for an explanation.

"He forgot the doughnuts" was all Charlie provided before heading after his partner.

Grady didn't say a word as he settled in behind his desk, picked up a stack of pink message slips, and started going through them, reading each and then relegating it to one of the neat piles he laid out in front of him according to importance and need for action.

Charlie waited until Grady took a sip of hot, black coffee before he casually ventured, "So, who is she, anyway?"

Grady's coffee sloshed down his front and he swiped at it futilely with his hand. "Shut up, Charlie, or I'm gonna rearrange your face."

"Touchy, aren't we?"

"She called me a 'sex-starved, adolescent pervert' and threatened to run me over with her car."

"You obviously made a spectacular first impression." Charlie considered the woman's charge and wondered what the devil had happened. "That doesn't sound like you at all, though. For God's sake, you're—"

"I said, I don't want to talk about it."

Charlie didn't doubt the truth of that claim for an instant. If, after the five long years since his wife's death, Grady was finally showing signs of life, this sudden change was bound to be a bit unsettling. As it was, it was already far past time he got back into the game. It wasn't normal or healthy for a thirty-nine-year-old man to shut himself off from everything but work and raising a daughter that was most of the way raised. Wisely keeping these observations to himself for the time being, Charlie changed the subject to what he truly believed was less sensitive territory: "You want lunch at McDonald's or Burger King?"

"Burger King."

ON THE DRIVE HOME from the police station, Hilary fumed impotently at her own inability to recognize a dire omen when she saw one. In retrospect, it was all too clear that that was exactly what she'd had, the very first thing that morning, when she'd discovered that one of the dogs had mistaken her brand-new black suede Charles Jourdan pumps for chew toys. They'd cost a hundred and fifty dollars, she'd only worn them once, and their destruction had set the tone for her entire day.

The car hadn't wanted to start, and it had taken twenty minutes of determined tinkering and cursing to coax it to life. A good deal more cursing had followed during the rush-hour drive into Oakland and the subsequent hunt for a parking space reasonably near the university's English department, where she was a graduate student. She'd managed to get to her office just in time for the appointment she'd scheduled with one of the students from the intro-to-lit class she taught as part of her fellowship. The student, of course, had been a no-show. She'd made the effort for absolutely nothing.

Frustrated, she'd decided to make the best of things and had gone to the library to photocopy an article. She'd wanted to copy it the week before, but hadn't had enough change. Since that time, however, someone with a similar change dilemma—and fewer scruples than she—had torn it out of the journal. She'd then gone back to her office to call the author of one of the definitive books on her dissertation topic, only to discover that the man had died the night before. At that point, she had written off the day as a total loss and headed for home, with a quick stop at the supermarket on the way.

Then, though she hadn't imagined it possible, the situation had worsened—from very bad to downright abysmal, a condition brought about by her encounter with Grady Thompson.

Thank God, Paul was home.

Paul Novotny was the only person in the world to whom Hilary would consider telling the whole sordid story; he was the only one who could understand, better than any of her few female friends could. No one offered sympathy and perfect, freshly ground-and-brewed coffee like Paul. No one cooked and cleaned and mothered housemates like Paul. If he weren't gay, she would have begged him to marry her and take care of her for the rest of her life.

He listened patiently as she sputtered through the saga, limiting his comments during the telling to sympathetic clucks and shakes of his head. He waited a full thirty seconds after she was through before he looked at her and impatiently asked, "Well?"

"Well, what?"

"Is he going to call you?"

"Paul, haven't you been listening at all?" she wailed.

"Of course I have, darling. That's why I'm asking. You're attracted to him, aren't you?"

Hilary eyed him narrowly. The last person she'd expected to turn on her was Paul, because he knew as well as anyone that her attraction to Grady Thompson wasn't the issue; it was what was bound to follow that was the real problem. She lit her second cigarette since she'd begun, her eighth of that day, and though Paul didn't comment on it, his eyebrows shot eloquently upward. He didn't need to remind her that she hadn't had one for three weeks, until her encounter with Grady had sent her running for the comfort of nicotine.

"You said he's a real hunk, didn't you?"

"That's not what I said at all!"

Paul shrugged indifferently, demonstrating where she'd picked up the habit. "It's what you meant. So, go out with him. Once, just for me. You haven't been out on a real date in months—not since you broke off the engagement with . . . Who was it the last time?"

"You think it's such a good idea, you go out with him," she snapped testily.

"It doesn't sound like I'm his type."

She took another sip of coffee and tried to change the subject. "Is there any more carrot cake?"

He wagged his finger at her. "Don't be evasive, Ree. I know you too well for that."

"You gonna bring in the big guns? Tell Michael?" Michael Cassimatis was their other housemate.

"You've got it, toots."

That's what Hilary was afraid of. When the pair of them got together, they could convince her that the moon was made of green cheese and the earth was flat. "Okay, Paul. Will it make you happy if I admit I think he's really attractive?"

"Will you admit you're hot for him?" Paul grinned wickedly.

"Do Mack trucks fly?"

"I didn't think you would." He frowned as if he was going to sulk indefinitely but then immediately brightened. "I suppose you're ready for some cheering up."

"There's more carrot cake?"

"Better than that. You got a package today that has foreign stamps and squiggles all over it."

"From Mom?" she asked expectantly, presenting him with her first real smile since she'd gotten home.

"I guess it must be." He shrugged again. "I can't read Chinese, you know."

Hilary's father, an executive with Easterbrook Appliances, had been selected to head the corporation's Asian operations in Taiwan five years earlier. While the distant assignment meant that she and her parents didn't get to see or talk to each other on any regular basis, it had its compensations for the whole family—chief among them that her mother could shop to her heart's content, her father could afford it, and she could open the frequent air-mail packages that came for her, filled with the plunder of her mother's most recent conquest.

When Paul produced the package—as well as a piece of carrot cake he'd been hoarding in some secret location in the back of the refrigerator—they were both delighted to discover that her mother's latest acquisition on her behalf had been a cheongsam. Those body-hugging, high-collared silk dresses had always made some secret, unliberated part of Hilary's soul think yearningly about emulating Mata Hari.

As they were admiring the brightly-colored, hand-stitched embroidery that embellished the front of the dress—and ruing the fact that the shipping had left it too wrinkled to wear without a trip to the dry cleaners—the telephone rang. Hilary nearly jumped through the ceiling, fearing that the moment of reckoning—the telephone call from Grady—had come. Left to her own devices, she would have given him a definite, indisputable no, but with Paul there, she didn't stand a chance of making her own decision; she would be forced to agree to see him.

It was Ryan. Hilary sighed with relief. Ryan Jenkins, a running back with the Pittsburgh Titans, had been one of the housemates' closest friends for several years, since shortly after they'd moved in together. Because all three were social creatures by nature—and involved in very different pursuits—the vast network of friends they'd collectively accumulated could best be described as eclectic, though there were some who alleged that eccentric was a more accurate way of putting it.

"Hi, doll. How you doing?" His deep baritone rang through the telephone's receiver. "All ready for the big party tonight? Bail that sexy dress of yours out of the cleaners?"

Hilary laughed. "Better than that—I bought a new one."

"Slit down to the navel or up to the . . ."

"Neither. It just fits like a second skin. Black. Sequins."

"Fit to make the eleven o'clock news?"

"Exactly," she assured him. "It's knock-'em-dead perfect."


WHEN GRADY GOT HILARY'S address and telephone number from the clerk, he briefly considered calling her, but decided to wait. With Charlie at the next desk, conditions weren't exactly ideal for cajoling her into going out with him, and he was sure that was exactly what he was going to have to do. Sighing, he stuck the slip of paper into his wallet and reached for a stack of messages that had to be taken care of before he and Charlie went home at the end of their shift.

"So, you gonna call her, or what?" Charlie asked curiously.

Grady stared at him levelly, but didn't answer the question.

"Well?"

"Don't you have something better to do than drive me crazy?"

"No."

"Then, find something."

"It's been slow around here," Charlie groused. "Don't you read the statistics? Crime's down twenty-three percent."

"You're complaining?"

"I'm afraid they'll stick me with the Liberty Avenue detail." Liberty Avenue was Pittsburgh's black eye. Right in the middle of the new, revitalized Golden Triangle, it was a six-block stretch of massage parlors and porn shows that every mayor for the past thirty years had sworn to eradicate. So far, the skin trade was winning the battle. "Jenny'd kill me."

Jenny was Charlie's wife.

"Then, I'd have something to investigate."

Charlie grumbled something under his breath and began shuffling papers. He stopped to peer at one of the photographs before handing it over to Grady. "Did you see this?"

Grady took it from him, looked at it, and shook his head. "Ryan Jenkins." He identified the man in the picture with no difficulty. "Any particular reason you've got this?"

Charlie leafed through the contents of the accompanying folder. "Looks like some sort of blackmail probe."

Grady reached across the desk for the folder and skimmed through it. According to the report, Jenkins had been paying money to blackmailers for almost a year, until they had approached him about shaving points during games. At that time, deciding the whole thing had gone far enough, he had come to the police for assistance. "Notice something missing here?"

"You mean, like a reason for the extortion?"

"Exactly. I wonder why they didn't ask when they took the initial report."

Charlie shook his head and shrugged. "Got me. Maybe they just didn't want to put it on paper at this point."

"Could be. I guess they decided it was too easy for things like that to get into the wrong hands."

"Yeah." Charlie sighed. "But if they'd written it down, at least now we'd know what Ryan Jenkins's deep, dark secret is."

THE FOLLOWING DAY, Grady and Charlie watched warily as their boss, Lieutenant Angelucci, paced up and down in front of his desk, as silent and ominous as a big cat on the prowl. Like his feline counterpart, he made the entire department apprehensive when he got like this.

"This case has to be handled with a certain amount of tact," Angelucci said in a voice so low, both detectives had to strain to hear. He paused mid-step, long enough to have them waiting on the edges of their seats for him to start moving again . . . or pounce on some unsuspecting prey. "Jenkins is a celebrity—national, not just local—and we can't go barging in, asking a lot of indiscreet questions, or the whole thing's gonna blow up in our faces."

Charlie sighed and asked, "How're we supposed to investigate this if Jenkins won't cooperate? After all, he's the one who filed the complaint—"

"But," Grady interrupted, "he won't tell anybody what he's being blackmailed for."

"What are we supposed to do? Go out and pick random suspects off the street?" Charlie continued, the touch of sarcasm in his voice revealing his frustration. "That'd be really productive."

"You know Amos Frazier's a big name in Pittsburgh, and not just because he owns the Titans," the lieutenant pointed out. "Economically and politically, he's got a lot of clout."

Both detectives nodded.

"All I'm asking is for you to give me something to take to the commissioner, so *he* has something to take back to Frazier. If Jenkins won't cooperate with us, there's not a lot we can do. Talk to Jenkins and his girlfriend. See where it goes—if it does go anywhere, that is."

Grady groaned quietly, as did Charlie. They both hated dead-end assignments that accomplished nothing except wasting time, and that's what this one looked like. It was apparent that Angelucci thought the same thing.

"You won't be able to talk to Jenkins until Tuesday. He's in Los Angeles for a Monday-night game. Go see the girl-friend."

"Who is she?" Charlie asked.

Angelucci looked down at the folder and shuffled through it before cursing softly and shaking his head. "It figures.... Her name's not in here, either. The assistant commissioner said she lives in that converted firehouse out in Regent Square. She's supposed to be some sort of host-ess or something. I understand she met Jenkins when she arranged a party for him."

Grady glanced at Charlie. Hostess. *That* figured, too.

An hour later, as they stood on the doorstep of the con-verted firehouse, Charlie commented casually, "You know, I passed this building on my way to work every day while they were doing the conversion. I always wondered who bought it."

"It makes perfect sense that someone like Jenkins's mis-tress would. Who else would do such a ridiculous thing?"

"It seems a little big for one person, doesn't it?"

"She probably needs all that space for wild parties," Grady grumbled. "That is, if a 'hostess' has real parties at all." The disparaging tone of his voice left no doubt as to exactly what he believed a hostess did.

"Would you do me a favor?" Charlie returned with a martyred sigh. "Would you call that girl? I'd hate to have to ask for a new partner at this stage of the game, but you're getting to be a real son of a bitch to be around."

Grady shot him a glare, but Charlie took no offense. He'd known Grady too long not to recognize that this be-havior was an aberration. That awareness didn't mean he intended to let it continue until Grady faced the fact that he was still alive and not meant to live like a monk for the remainder of his life, in spite of the fact that his wife had died. Grady had met this girl two days ago, which was was plenty of time for him to make the adjustment, as far as Charlie was concerned. "I'm serious. When you called my house last night, you sounded like such a grouch that Jenny asked if you'd been getting enough—"

"You want to drop this?" Grady snapped.

"—roughage in your diet," Charlie completed unrepentantly.

"Like now?"

"All right, all right. Just settle down. Someone's coming."

The door opened to reveal a man lounging against the wall in an effeminate pose. "Yes?"

"We're police detectives. We're here to see . . ." Charlie paused, uncertain how to ask for a woman whose name he didn't know. Before he could continue floundering for an explanation, the other man spoke.

"Right. You're here to see Ree."

"We're here about the blackmail case," Grady clarified in a clipped voice.

"Surly, aren't we?" A perfectly arched eyebrow shot heavenward. "Perhaps one of you has some ID?"

Grady muttered something obscene under his breath and dug into his back pocket for his wallet. Charlie silently followed his lead and they handed over their badges.

He inspected them both before the eyebrow shot up again. "Grady Thompson?"

Grady reached for his wallet, grumbling again before he shoved it back into his hip pocket.

Charlie retrieved his own with a little more graciousness. "May we see her, please? That is, if she's home."

"Certainly. This should be interesting." He turned back into the hall, gesturing for them to follow.

He led them upstairs into a huge loftlike area that was the biggest, most spectacularly decorated living room Charlie had ever seen. A pair of cream leather sofas long enough to seat their entire squad bracketed a fantastic square faux-malachite cocktail table. Matching sofa tables stood behind each of the sofas, topped by a pair of cream-and-brass Art Deco lamps. Dominating the end wall was a huge modern oil painting that was at least six by six and was indisputably real. Charlie, who had spent the past three weekends shopping for new furniture with Jenny, knew the whole thing must have cost the moon.

As they continued to gape at the setting, the man moved to the bottom of a metal spiral staircase and yelled up, "Ree?"

"Don't bother, Paul," a deep masculine voice called back. "She's got her headphones on. I can hear her singing along."

"The detectives are here to talk to Ree about Ryan. Should I just send them up?"

Grady heard heavy footsteps clomp down the staircase and a bearded man came into view. Except for the tortoiseshell-framed glasses he wore, he looked like Hercules, at least the way he'd looked in a book of legends Grady had read to his daughter Stacy when she was younger. Hercules-with-Glasses shrugged in lazy response to the question. "I guess so. I've got to get going. If Christie calls, tell her I'm running late and on my way."

"Sure. Maybe you should meet them first, though."

"Paul, I really don't have time. I'm already late." He was almost to the door.

"It's Grady Thompson."

The big bearded head snapped around in response and he strode back into the room. "Grady Thompson?"

"Grady Thompson," Paul assured him gravely.

Unerringly, with no indication from Paul as to which of them was Grady, Hercules-with-Glasses walked up to Grady and peered at him curiously. The scrutiny unnerved Grady, but he did his best to meet the man, stare for stare.

"She's not gonna like this," the big man remarked, still studying Grady.

"I know," Paul replied, equally neutral.

"She's not gonna like this at all!" A huge grin appeared on the bearded face and a roar of laughter burst out, as he threw back his shaggy head in undisguised delight.

Paul leaned back against the wall, laughing with him.

Grady's mind raced furiously, trying to determine exactly how he had become the butt of a joke that he didn't understand. He'd never met the woman—why in God's name would it upset her that he was here to talk to her? More important, why did these two think it was so funny?

"Doesn't look like a pervert to me!" Hercules-with-Glasses exclaimed.

"A sex-starved, adolescent pervert!" Paul corrected.

Grady felt his face drain of color. "Where is she?"

Paul, still laughing, pointed up the spiral staircase. "All the way up."

Cursing under his breath, Grady bounded up the stairs two at a time.

Charlie, finally grasping the situation, asked quietly and hesitantly, "By chance, is Ree a blonde with a red Mazda?"

"You betcha!" the bearded man roared, dropping to the sofa and propping his feet up on the coffee table.

"I thought you had to leave," Paul reminded him, finally bringing his laughter under control.

"Not on your life! Christie can wait! I wouldn't miss this for the world!"

WHEN GRADY got to the top of the staircase, he was winded and dizzy—not from the physical exertion of the long spiral climb, but from the mental strain. Hilary Campbell's claim that "it wasn't a good idea" to go out with him had been an understatement of colossal proportions. Who was this woman anyway? He leaned on the metal railing and took deep breaths until he felt recovered and composed enough to move to the door of the room. Once there, he stopped as he confronted a sight that left him even more stunned and disoriented than he already was.

Sitting in the middle of the bed, surrounded by dogs and cats and blue college examination books, was a woman in a modest, full-skirted Laura Ashley dress that covered her legs completely to her toes, with a matching ribbon holding her hair back in a ponytail. Grady gaped at her, wondering how this sweet, wholesome girl had come to take the place of both the elusive vixen he remembered from the parking-lot debacle and the trashy broad he'd expected Ryan Jenkins's mistress to be.

Hilary didn't notice Grady's arrival. She was too engrossed in the indisputable evidence that the university's star fullback, Boone Fuller, was all brawn and no brain. "Crap," she muttered softly, closing her eyes and rubbing her fingertips against her temples in disgust.

*Not another one.* Why couldn't she get one of the student athletes who understood that the primary reason for going to college was supposed to be to study? Every time she got one of these midget-brained giants in her class, she ended up defending herself and her ethical standards to the football coach, the athletic director, the chancellor, several trustees, and at least one well-meaning alumnus contributor. The head of the English department, a dear, sweet invertebrate, would defend her, but God knew it wasn't worth anything.

In the end she'd have to tutor the jock, which amounted to dragging him bodily through the course so she could justify the C she finally gave him. She'd done it before, and it wasn't a pleasant prospect. A few of the jocks had treated the tutoring as if it were a joke, and a couple had even concluded that she could be "charmed" around to their way of thinking. Things had gotten a little out of hand once or twice, when their hormones had blocked out their ability to understand that "no" meant precisely that. When they'd been slow to get the point, first Michael and then her buddy Zeke, who was even larger than Michael, had appointed themselves bodyguards and gone along with her.

Irked by the thought of dealing with yet another of the school's overly exalted barbarians on a one-on-one basis, Hilary slapped the blue book onto the comforter, in a single sentence summing up her opinion of the athletic department and jocks in general.

The pithy outburst brought Grady back to earth with a thud. A quick glance around the room, in combination with the fluent profanity, reminded him precisely who and what Hilary Campbell was.

The shimmery black cocktail dress he'd seen in her car hung neatly from a bracket on the far wall, but everything else was as much a shambles as the back of her car had been. Tennis shoes battled for space next to satin spike heels. Lacy lingerie and sheer stockings were draped over furniture and hung out of half-open drawers. There was a heap of black leather he didn't want to think about tossed negligently in one corner.

Grady had always had a fundamental distaste for the people who regarded sex as a marketable commodity.

That a woman who was part of that world had fooled him into being attracted to her made him question his ability to judge character.

He should have heeded Charlie's advice that it was high time he started to get out and meet women again. Perhaps then, his brain wouldn't have short-circuited the moment he'd set eyes on her. He wouldn't have smashed up the T-Bird. He wouldn't have asked her out. He wouldn't have subjected himself to two solid days of wavering between anticipation and apprehension as he picked up the telephone, dialed the first six digits of her number and then hung up before dialing the last.

And he wouldn't have felt this keen sense of disappointment and regret—not just at the loss of something he'd never had, but at his own stupidity for wanting it.

Hilary finally felt the force of someone's eyes upon her and raised her head in response. Her eyes widened incredulously when she saw who it was. While she'd had a feeling that she hadn't heard the last of Grady Thompson, she'd expected their next encounter would be on the telephone rather than face-to-face.

As she slid the headphones down to dangle against her nape, she couldn't help thinking that he should have looked at least a little happy to see her. Instead, he regarded her with a thunderous look. Even the animals recognized the menace of it and performed a mass withdrawal to the lower region of the firehouse. If she had any sense at all, she'd be right behind them.

Sense had never, however, been her strong suit. "If you're here to arrest me for kidnapping the Lindbergh baby, I think I should mention that I've got an ironclad alibi."

"Why didn't you tell me you were a hook—"

"I am not," she declared, scrambling to her feet. She became tangled up in the cord of the headphones before she discarded them behind her on the bed. He didn't have to finish the word for her to know what he'd been about to say; she'd run across that mistaken impression of *hostess* before. Generally speaking, she found the error amusing, but, when Grady Thompson made it, it wasn't amusing at all.

"Don't hide behind euphemisms, Hilary—it's the same thing."

"It is not, Grady. I don't—"

"Liar," he accused.

"Pervert." It was a cheap shot, but it had practically become habit to think of Grady as "the pervert." Her use of the word was pure reflex.

It was a bad one. Grady exploded. "I am *not* a pervert!"

"And I am *not* a liar!"

His voice dropped to a more civilized level, but his accusations continued. "You said you wouldn't go out with me because it wouldn't be a good idea. . . ."

Her voice lowered, too. "It's true!"

"But that's not the real reason, is it? The truth of the matter is, you wouldn't go out with me because I can't afford you!"

"No! That's not it!"

Grady hesitated for a moment, grappling with the inherent discrepancy between her expression of wounded innocence and her collection of black leather. He didn't know why, but he wanted to believe her—almost as much as he wanted to help her put the leather to good use. "It's not?"

"That's not it at all," she insisted, shaking her head in denial. As she looked into his eyes, she took one step nearer, reached out, and touched his arm.

Before he had time to realize what he was doing, Grady closed the distance between them with a single stride, slipped his arms around her waist and towed her up against the hard length of his body. Though her hands, trapped between them, pressed against his chest, Hilary did not resist the embrace, not even when his arms gathered more purposefully around her and his head bent toward hers with single-minded determination.

Hilary groaned softly—a sound that was more like a prayer than a protest.

Grady lowered his head until his mouth brushed across hers. It was a tentative touch, one that sought permission rather than demanded compliance.

She granted it; more than that, she encouraged it. Her parted lips stayed open, inviting him to align their mouths in a more intimate fashion. Her hands, still braced against his chest, relaxed, allowing the shallow hollows of her palms to conform to the contours of his pectoral muscles. Her feet stole another inch or two forward, insinuating themselves between his and bringing their hips and thighs in direct contact.

Everything that happened after that was lost in a haze of pure sensation whose effects he'd completely forgotten. At some point, her arms moved up to encircle his neck, her mouth opened wider to receive him, and her tongue moved to parry with his. As she responded to him, he clutched her more closely, molding their bodies together and fitting the evidence of his desire against her softness. Both breathed heavily, their hearts beat together in a rapid cadence, and the moan they shared could have come from either of them.

It was that sound of unmistakable arousal that made Grady realize exactly what he was doing—or, rather, what *they* were doing together. Next came the awful realization that he liked it a lot more than he should. Despite Hilary's repeated denials—and despite the devastating impact she had on both his senses and his good sense—he didn't believe she was innocent, and he was appalled with himself for wishing he could.

As he snatched his mouth away from hers and released her, he knew he had to get away from her immediately. Backing slowly toward the door, he kept a careful watch on her the whole way, even though he knew it was himself he really had to worry about. When he got there, he spun on his heel and headed down the stairs, muttering a steady stream of vicious curses that were directed much more at himself than at her.

IN THE LIVING ROOM below, Hilary's two housemates watched as Charlie groaned and buried his face in his hands. "God, he's not gonna be happy about this...."

"I thought he wanted to go out with Ree," Paul commented with more than a little confusion.

"He didn't know she was ..." Charlie shook his head wearily. "He didn't know she was Jenkins's mist—"

"Hilary?"

"Hilary?"

The two men asked the incredulous question simultaneously.

"Don't you police do your research?"

"Excuse me?" Charlie asked. The whole scene was more than he could comprehend.

"You thought Ree was Jenkins's mistress, didn't you?" Paul asked, coming right to the point.

Charlie nodded helplessly. "She isn't?"

"Hilary?"

"Hilary?" Michael shook his head and laughed, as if he knew something that made the notion ridiculous.

"For all we know, she's a virgin," Paul added ingenuously.

"Paul, really." Michael gave him an glare of reprimand.

"All right, maybe I'm wrong," Paul added, deliberately misunderstanding his housemate.

Charlie gaped at them both, thoroughly bewildered. Why were these two crazy men telling him these things?

"I can't tell you how relieved we were to hear she's found a live one this time."

"What?" Charlie felt as if he were playing straight man for the Abbott and Costello "Who's on first?" routine.

"The caveman bit was sheer brilliance. Me Tarzan, you Jane'll do it every time. Even if she won't admit it, she loved it. It was quite a change from the spineless wonders she usually digs up."

"Caveman?"

"It isn't every day someone throws you over his shoulder and carts you off." Paul sighed sadly. "More's the pity."

"Grady?"

Michael started to laugh at Charlie's apparent astonishment. "That's the way we hear it."

"Grady Thompson? Grady Thompson threw somebody over his shoulder?"

"Not somebody. Ree."

"Some people have all the luck." Paul shook his head and sighed again.

"She probably wouldn't have been so mad if he weren't a groper." Michael chuckled again.

"A groper?" Charlie's head was reeling. This was all more than he could handle. "Grady? Grady's not like that!"

Paul shrugged. "I told her his hand probably slipped when he tried to pull down her skirt."

Michael nodded in agreement. "Probably."

"Pull down her skirt?" Charlie held his temples in place, trying to prevent his brain from escaping.

He never got an answer, because, at just that moment, Grady came pounding down the stairs, the look on his face a curious blend of furious, appalled, and shaken. He stopped in the living room only long enough to hold out one hand and demand, "Keys!" in a voice that would have stopped Godzilla dead in his tracks. Then he stormed out.

He had already left the building before Charlie realized he had just been stranded in the middle of Psychiatric Central.

# 3

FOR A MOMENT, Charlie nearly panicked, until he remembered that Lieutenant Angelucci knew where he was. He was relatively sure that when Grady arrived back at the station without him, his boss would send someone to rescue him. Meanwhile, there didn't seem to be any reason he couldn't take a statement from Hilary himself. He said as much to her two housemates and then added, "That is, of course, if she's in any better shape to talk lucidly than my partner."

"I wouldn't count on it," Michael cautioned him.

He was right. When Hilary stormed down the stairs a moment later, the steam radiated from her much as it had from Grady. Charlie noted, however, that the first thing she did was look around the room for Grady, and she didn't appear to be hoping he was gone. "Calling me a—" She stopped abruptly to peer at Charlie. "Who are you?"

"The pervert's partner," Michael answered equanimically.

"Charlie Landis," he introduced himself, holding out his hand.

Hilary ignored the cordial gesture. "How do you work with that man? He's . . ." She went on to insult Grady and his antecedents back to Adam.

Charlie gaped at her, stunned by her assessment of Grady's character.

"I guess you can tell Thompson made a spectacular first impression," Michael commented wryly to Charlie.

"A second one, too, by the looks of it," Paul contributed.

"I don't understand it," Charlie murmured. "This isn't like Grady. He's usually so sensible, so—"

"Lord, no!" Hilary groaned. "Not again! Not another one! Do you hear me?" She shook her finger demandingly, first at Michael and then at Paul. "I knew it! I just knew it!"

Both men simply smiled.

Charlie's head began to reel again, not that it had stopped completely from before, when he had been talking to just Michael and Paul.

"Tell me . . ." she began, and Charlie flinched reflexively, realizing that he had become the focus of her attention. "Where does Grady live?"

"Live?" Charlie echoed. "You mean his address?"

"No. What section of the city? What's his house like?"

Automatically, still not certain where the conversation was going, Charlie replied, "Highland Park. He has one of those big Dutch colonials over—"

"See?" she asked her housemates, who appeared to understand her point. "What'd I tell you?"

Absolutely positive he was missing something vital and wanting to know what it was, Charlie maintained his silence while the tumult roiled around him. It didn't make sense, but then maybe his brain was just fried by the entire afternoon. He wondered if things were usually this bizarre around here, or if Hilary's latest confrontation with Grady was to blame. Eventually, from the acclimated expressions of her housemates, he concluded that Hilary Campbell was like the eye of a hurricane—things around her just naturally became agitated. Including

Grady, he thought. In fifteen years, he'd never seen Grady—good old sensible-as-white-bread Grady—so out of control, so utterly...*not* Grady. What this tiny woman did to his partner amazed him.

In all the confusion, no one but Charlie heard the doorbell. Given the choice between interrupting the three housemates or answering the door himself, he opted for the relative safety of the door.

It was Grady who must have finally realized that not only did he have Charlie's car but he'd left Charlie behind. Charlie was torn between relief that he hadn't been abandoned and dread that Grady's return would set off a whole new round of pandemonium.

"Hi, Grady," he said warily, testing those waters before he allowed him back into the firehouse.

"What's the fuss about?" Grady looked up the hallway in the direction of the racket and then started toward it.

Charlie stopped him. "I'm not sure, but I think it has something to do with you. You wanna tell me about it?"

"I can't stand it," Grady admitted wretchedly. "I wrecked the T-Bird and—"

"Grady, you don't know—"

"—she made a fool out of me and—"

"Grady, pal, listen to me—"

"—dammit, I can't help it, but she *still* does something to me!" He dropped his forehead against the wall with a thump.

"Grady... Grady, please... Listen to me." Taking advantage of Grady's silence and bowed head, Charlie went on. "You're *wrong* about her. She and Jenkins are nothing more than friends."

Grady's head shot up and he peered at Charlie intently. "Friends? Hilary and a rich, good-looking jock like Jenkins? Get serious."

"I *am* serious. While you were upstairs, I had a talk with those two guys she lives with and they told me she and Ryan Jenkins were never anything more than friends."

Raking his fingers through his hair, Grady looked at his partner through haunted eyes. "Then why did everybody *think* she was his mistress?"

Charlie shrugged. "Got me. But they seemed sure about it."

A faint glimmer of hope lit Grady's eyes. "How sure?"

"Real sure. As if they knew something they weren't going to tell me."

The glimmer grew, flickering hopefully, like a fledgling fire with a new infusion of kindling.

"And 'hostess' means exactly that."

The flame appeared as if it might have a chance to thrive.

"Nothing more. She arranges parties—cocktail parties, receptions, that kind of thing—for people who don't want to do it themselves or don't have the time. A pretty lucrative business, I understand."

"Oh, God . . ."

"Arranges caterers, entertainment . . ."

"Oh, God, Charlie. The things I said . . ."

"You've got a lot of fence-mending to do, pal."

"I know it."

"Did you really throw her over your shoulder and grope?"

"Yes." Grady's face wore a pained expression.

"Oh, Lord . . ."

Grady closed his eyes and gulped. Then he described in detail the rest of that eventful morning. He came to the part about taking his wallet out of his pocket, when Charlie interrupted.

"They weren't still in there," he said with dread in his voice. The Saturday before, Charlie had all but forced Grady out on a blind date with one of Jenny's friends and handed the condoms to him, joking, "Just in case."

"Oh, yes, they were."

Charlie filled in the missing pieces, tried to stifle a laugh, and failed miserably.

"It's not funny."

"Oh, yes, it is. If you weren't so uptight, you'd think so, too." Charlie's laughter reached full fruition. He guessed he'd been pretty accurate in his judgment that Grady was finally ready to start dating. What he'd been mistaken about was his estimation of what kind of woman would interest Grady. He'd been thinking about someone a little older, a little more settled and a *lot* less flamboyant than Hilary. Obviously, he'd been wrong.

"I am *not* uptight."

"Grady, you're my best friend, but you're the most annoyingly uptight human being I know. You ought to loosen up more often."

"If that's loosening up, I hope to God it never happens again."

Still shaking his head and laughing, Charlie turned in the direction of the living room. "I'd like to discuss it with you, Grady, but some other time. What we really ought to do is take her statement so we can get back to the station."

Grady nodded reluctantly.

They went back up the hallway to the living room.

When Hilary saw Charlie, she smiled ingenuously. "Oh, you're back. If you're ready to take my statement now—"

"Hilary, I'm sorry."

Hilary hadn't seen Grady before she heard his voice, and she drew in a startled gasp as her eyes flew up to meet his.

"What are you doing back here?"

Grady flinched at the rancor in her voice, even as he told himself he deserved it. He'd said such horrible things to her. He should have had the decency to let her explain. He shouldn't have kissed her. Worst of all, he shouldn't have reacted with such undisguised horror when he'd felt them both responding to that kiss.

He was an idiot, a first-class jerk. He still wanted her, and she looked at him as if he were pond scum. Charlie was absolutely right; he did have a lot of fences to mend. Mend, hell—he was going to have to tear them down and start over again from scratch.

He recognized that the emotion that had fueled the exchange upstairs was jealousy, even though it didn't make a damn bit of sense. He'd only met her a few days before, after all. But he thought about it for a minute and knew it was true. While Hilary Campbell wasn't exactly his—or anybody else's—idea of wife material, she was certainly the first woman who had really sparked his interest since he'd gotten over losing Anne.

The important question now was, what was he going to do about it? He couldn't just ignore it and go on with his life. He had to change her mind, had to explore what it was about Hilary that made him act as if he'd lost his mind. Had to find out why, in God's name, he *liked* it. And that meant he had to change her opinion of him, which he was sure couldn't sink much lower than it already was. And he had to start now.

Grady took Hilary by the elbow and gently propelled her through the swinging door and into the kitchen, away from their fascinated audience.

"Hilary..." he tried, but she didn't hear him. She couldn't, because of her furious litany.

He swung her around to face him and put one hand over her mouth to stop her.

She squawked indignantly against the muzzle and then gave up, though her eyes continued to burn with bright blue fire.

"I'm sorry."

Hilary relaxed almost imperceptibly. It wasn't much, but it was a start.

"I never should have said those things to you."

A bit more of the tension left her body, and he felt secure enough to remove his hand from her mouth.

"They're not true. None of it's true." For reasons Hilary didn't understand, it seemed important to make him believe that.

"Even if any of it was, I had no right to say it."

Though she recognized that it was supposed to be an apology, the implication that he didn't entirely believe her business was a legitimate one was still there. She was seized by a maniacal urge to club him in the side of the head so hard it would make his ears ring—and, maybe, drive the truth into his thick skull. What stopped her from doing just that was the expression on his face. The poor man looked as if someone already *had* hit him—right between the eyes.

It was a familiar enough expression, making her feel as if she'd delivered the blow. With a gasp, she turned and fled from the room.

ONCE SHE WAS UPSTAIRS in her bedroom, Hilary dug the pack of cigarettes out of her pocket and lit one with shaking hands. She knew she was smoking nearly as much as she had before quitting, but she'd never been good at handling tension. Lord knew, she had plenty of reason to be tense these days: the unforeseen complications of her and Ryan's masquerade; the major altercation that was going to erupt when she returned Boone Fuller's latest exam (which hadn't even been within hailing distance of passing); and the realization that Grady Thompson's attraction to her wasn't going to go away quietly—primarily because the attraction was mutual.

It was a mess. But then, most things in her life usually were. Her personal life, that is. Academically and professionally, she was generally acknowledged to be the English department's hottest new talent, a top-notch researcher and teacher, but personally... Well, "a bit of a shambles" accurately described the normal state of her personal life.

Although her roommates joked about it, and she laughed along with the jokes, it wasn't really funny, as far as she was concerned. Seven fiancés. All sensible, stable men. She'd driven each and every one of them stark raving mad, until they'd been forced to break off the engagements in order to save the last, lingering vestiges of their sanity. To her own credit, she hadn't parted on bad terms with any of them; she still considered each a friend. The fact of the matter was that none of them had been able to face the prospect of living with her, in utter chaos, for the rest of his life.

Actually, that was how she'd hooked up with Paul and Michael in the first place. She'd been on the rebound from ... fiancé number three? Maybe four? She'd needed a place to live and Michael, whose wife had just decided a man with an American Express gold card was more attractive than a struggling artist, had offered her the spare room in the apartment where he'd lived at that time. Shortly afterward, Paul, who'd just broken up with his lover, Marshall, had moved in with them. The crowded situation had eventually led to the purchase of the firehouse. Being housemates had given the two men ample opportunity to be firsthand observers of the last several engagements. Both of them knew, every bit as well as she did, the need for her to avoid romantic entanglements, because when she got involved with someone, too many people—particularly her—got hurt.

After the last engagement—to Jack—had ended in the usual ignominious fashion, they'd arrived at the perfect solution to her dilemma: Ryan Jenkins, the definitive rich, handsome, athletic, eligible bachelor. Women pursued him incessantly, lusting after his body almost as much as they desired his status and money. If she and Ryan pretended to be lovers, it would solve both of their problems at once. It prevented her from getting involved with anyone. It discouraged women from chasing Ryan and at the same time, didn't allow anyone to know the truth: that Ryan and Paul were lovers.

And that fact, of course, was the basis for the extortion that had brought Grady Thompson to the firehouse.

Why couldn't they have assigned the case to someone else? Whatever happened to nice, near-retirement-age cops whose only interest in her was in what she could tell them about who might be blackmailing Ryan? Where was Karl Malden when she needed him?

Hilary wasn't exactly certain what had possessed her the other day when she'd told Grady she wasn't seeing anyone—she had never hesitated to use her alleged relationship with Ryan as a smokescreen before. Who would have expected that telling the truth was going to backfire on her in quite the way it had that afternoon?

At first she'd thought Grady's assumption that she was a hooker might mean the end of the interest he'd shown in her; that belief had only lasted until he'd given her a kiss that had shaken her right down to her toes. Grady had felt it, too, even if he'd been appalled when he realized what was happening.

She'd been more apprehensive than appalled, but then, she was the one with the experience to know better. For the good of both of them, she was just going to have to stay as far away from Grady Thompson as humanly possible.

"THOMPSON SPEAKING." Several days later, Grady answered the telephone in their office at the precinct station.

"Grady Thompson?" a man on the other end asked. His voice sounded vaguely familiar, but Grady couldn't imagine why.

"Yes?" Grady returned.

"This is Paul Novotny...Hilary Campbell's housemate?" he added as a means of clarification.

"I remember." Not only did Grady remember the owner of the voice, but the whole bizarre afternoon at the firehouse came back to him in a humiliating rush. He'd been meaning to call Hilary since then, but mortification had stopped him every time he'd picked up the phone.

"I didn't know who else to call. Are you still handing Ryan Jenkins's case?"

"Yes." What there was of it, since Jenkins hadn't told them anything constructive before he'd gone to Dallas for another away game. He and Charlie had consoled themselves—and Lieutenant Angelucci—with the reminder that the next two games were both at home. "Do you have some more information for me?"

"I thought you should know...I went over to Ryan's house to pick up his mail and found a note threatening Ree. And, after getting her tires slashed the other night—"

"What?" Grady almost shouted, coming to his feet.

Across the desk, Charlie looked up from the report he was reading and stared at Grady.

"Is she okay?" Grady demanded. "Nothing's happened to her, right?"

"She's fine, and so is the car, now that it's gotten new tires. She doesn't even know about the note yet, and neither does Ryan, because I called you right away."

"What's it say?"

"Not much, really. Just that if he didn't go along with them and start shaving points on games, they were going to go after his girl."

Grady thought about it for a moment, recalling that Hilary had told him she and Jenkins were only friends. "But—"

"Look, we both know she's not really Ryan's girlfriend, but they *think* she is."

"Where is she now?"

"She's still over at the university, because she's got class until five."

Grady glanced at his watch. It was just after four, which gave him almost an hour to get there. Plenty of time, since his police marker meant he didn't have to worry about finding a parking place once he got there. "Pack up some things for her and Charlie'll come by and get them." He looked across the desk and Charlie nodded in silent confirmation. "He'll get the note then, too, so we can take a look at it. I'll need directions to where she is at the university."

Paul provided them for him.

"Don't worry about it—I'll take care of her."

After Paul thanked him, Grady hung up the telephone and looked at Charlie.

"That was Hilary's Campbell's roommate."

"Which one?"

"Paul. He said the blackmailers sent a note to Jenkins threatening to hurt Hilary if he doesn't do what they want." He edged around the desk and grabbed his jacket off the rack. "I'm gonna go and get her at school after she finishes class for the day. Give him some time to pack her a bag before you go over there. I'll see you back at my house later."

"Your house?" Charlie echoed.

"You know there's not enough money allocated for safe houses, and this case isn't nearly hairy enough to warrant one, even if they did slash the tires on her car the other night."

Charlie nodded.

"I just want to get her out of the firehouse for a while until we establish whether or not there's a real danger."

Charlie nodded again.

"And I want her where I can keep an eye on her," Grady finished as he went out the door.

"Sure, you do," Charlie said to himself with a smile as he crumpled up the paper he'd just finished reading and tossed it into the wastebasket. It was a department memo about random vandalism on several dozen cars parked in the university's parking lots.

WHEN HILARY EMERGED from her Romanticism seminar, Grady was waiting for her in the hall. Forgetting all about William Blake and nineteenth-century mysticism, she glared at him and asked, "You're back again?"

He took her arm and led her into a nearby alcove.

"What are you arresting me for *this* time? The Great Train Robbery?"

"I'm not arresting you. I'm taking you into custody."

"Fine distinction," she commented wryly.

"Ryan Jenkins got a note today threatening *you* if he doesn't go along with the blackmailers."

"Me?" A moment later, after she had a chance to remember it, she added, "But Ryan's out of town."

"Paul called me." Quickly he related his conversation with her housemate.

"So where are you taking me?"

"My house." He hauled her out of the alcove and started down the hall to the elevators.

Panic-stricken by the prospect, she dug in her heels and tried to pull him to a halt. "Your house? No way, Grady."

"I don't have a choice, Hilary." He reiterated all of the rationales he'd told Charlie earlier. "I just want you to be safe." His voice cracked with emotion. "I couldn't stand to see you get hurt."

Absorbing his concern for her, Hilary finally nodded. Even as she did, she knew it was a mistake. She didn't have the slightest doubt that Grady Thompson posed a far greater danger to her than Ryan's blackmailers did.

"My car's near the Mazda, so you can follow me to my house," he instructed.

"You got back the Thunderbird?" After Michael had explained to her that the car was practically a legend among vintage car buffs, she recognized, if not exactly understood, his unnatural attachment to it.

"No." He shook his head sadly. "My other car. The Clunker, the one I drive in bad weather."

Less than fifteen minutes later, Hilary pulled into the driveway behind Grady's car, which turned out not to be exactly the "clunker" he'd called it. In truth, it was a police-issue, three-year-old Plymouth sedan—the kind of sensible vehicle she'd have expected a man like Grady to drive.

Grady's house was also exactly what she'd expected, just as Charlie had begun to describe it to her that day at the firehouse: a two-story Dutch colonial with a perfectly groomed and landscaped lawn, between two more just like it on a quiet street with trees.

She groaned inwardly. By all appearances, Grady fit the profile even more closely than she had feared. He could have been cut from the same mold as each and every one of her doomed fiancés.

He got out of his car, came over to hers, and opened the door for her. As she got out, he asked her hopefully, "So, what do you think?"

Hilary followed him around the gas grill and the redwood picnic table to the atrium door. "It's the middle-class dream house."

Grady peered at her curiously, uncertain what she meant by the remark, which sounded more like an insult than a compliment. "Stacy's probably already home. She's my daughter."

As they entered through the atrium door, Hilary found herself in a sunny breakfast room attached to the huge country-style kitchen. Seated on a stool, cutting up tomatoes and cucumbers as she spoke into the telephone receiver tucked between her ear and shoulder, was a pretty dark-haired girl in her mid-teens.

This was Grady's daughter? She was sitting down, but Hilary could still tell that the girl was taller than she was. Somehow, she'd had a six- or seven-year-old in mind.

The girl quickly got off the telephone, and Grady introduced them. Although Stacy's greeting was friendly, Hilary was so overwhelmed by the afternoon's series of events—beginning with Grady's unexpected arrival at the university and ending with the even-more-unexpected discovery that he had a daughter this age—that she wasn't quite sure how to react to anything.

"You look like you could use a drink."

"I could." Actually, she could use several.

He turned toward the refrigerator and she watched as well-defined muscles rippled under the cloth of his shirt. "Beer or wine or something mixed?"

"Beer's fine." It took every ounce of willpower Hilary had to keep her voice steady as she remembered the way that hard body had felt against hers when he'd kissed her. Lord, she was in *very* big trouble.

Later, during dinner, Grady's determined efforts to be polite and solicitous alternately attracted and unnerved Hilary. Stacy attentively watched the whole show, bemused and amused as only a fifteen-year-old girl could be by the sudden revelation that her father might possess another male identity besides "Daddy." Her fascination with the subject didn't last long enough to suit Hilary, however. Almost as soon as they had finished eating, a telephone call from one of her friends sent her scurrying from the house, leaving Hilary and Grady entirely alone. Suddenly the large barn of a house seemed smaller, more intimate. Hilary didn't like it a bit—especially not when Grady was acting so amiable. As she'd recognized during the drive from the supermarket to the police station a few days before, a friendly Grady Thompson was a far more attractive—and unnerving—commodity than an irritated one.

"Let's take our coffee into the family room," he suggested. "It's more comfortable in there."

"Okay," she replied, her voice as deliberately indifferent as she could manage. She would have preferred taking her coffee all the way back to the firehouse, particularly when she saw there were no chairs in the room, just a huge sectional sofa. No avoiding him there. She waited for him to sit down first, and then sat as far away as she could get and still be in the same room.

Her conspicuous effort to avoid him bothered Grady immensely. Though he'd been on his best behavior, conducting himself like the reasonable, rational, adult human being he actually was—not like the sex-starved adolescent pervert she'd called him at first—she still acted as if she was a lot more worried about being alone with him in his house than she was about the threat that had brought her there.

Come to think of it, she really hadn't seemed all that concerned by the threat, in spite of the fact that she'd been the target of it. Most people would have been shaking in their shoes. The part of his mind that had spent fifteen years on the police force couldn't help wondering why.

"You know, Hilary, you're taking this whole mess pretty well," he commented. Because he was fishing for any information she might be able to give him, he did his best to make it sound like a casual remark, rather than an accusation.

"Exactly which mess are you talking about?"

"All of them, actually. The extortion, the threats. . . ."

"Well, it's been going on for so long, we've all had time to get used to the idea of someone blackmailing Ryan . . ." Grady must have looked alarmed at the admission, because she hastily added, "Not used to it as in ignoring it, or saying it doesn't matter, but the way someone gets used to a chronic illness—or a policeman gets used to—"

"Seeing murder and mayhem on a regular basis," he completed with a nod. He knew what she meant. If he hadn't become inured to it years before, he wouldn't have been able to continue.

"Exactly. Ryan never would have come to you at all if they hadn't wanted him to start shaving points on games. He couldn't do it, and we all thought . . ."

Her voice trailed off and he prompted, "Thought what, Hilary?"

"That, eventually, they'd just stop and go away."

"Blackmailers don't usually do that. They always come back, asking for more." He shook his head and sighed. "Would Jenkins have kept paying if they hadn't?"

She nodded in silent reply.

"Even with the threats?"

She shrugged and fluttered her hands, looking so endearing and vulnerable that he wanted to hold her, protect her. He'd noticed he often felt that way—between bouts of wanting to seduce or throttle her. "We'd all kind of hoped that going to the police would be enough to make it stop, but I think that's what actually prompted the threat. They know he can't shave points for them now, because it's on record that somebody wanted him to. I think they're getting desperate."

"Do you think you know who 'they' are?" he asked carefully, trying to conceal the unmitigated horror he felt at the word *desperate*. Desperate men were capable of anything, as he'd seen more times than he cared to remember.

She shook her head. "We all thought . . ." she said, before stopping and stiffening.

"Thought what?" Grady pressed. When she didn't answer him, he asked, "What do they have on him, Hilary?"

"I can't tell you that, Grady."

"Can't? Or won't?"

"Both. Don't ask me. Please."

The detective inside him struggled with the man. The detective insisted he pursue whatever it was Hilary was hiding. The man, on the other hand, didn't want to alienate her. Compromising, they agreed to give it another shot at some future time. "About this hostessing business . . ."

"You know, don't you, Grady, that hostess meant just that? All I did was organize and give parties. Period."

He'd been about to tell her that until this was over, she was out of business, but he nodded in understanding.

Hilary peered at him for a moment, until she decided he really believed her. "You'd be surprised what people will pay not to have to do these things for themselves. Being in grad school, I needed a way to make money without it taking a lot of time. I found out organizing parties was something I was good at, and one job just followed another, as people heard about what I did."

"You have to know a lot of people to make something like that work, don't you?" Grady put his arm around her shoulder and Hilary felt a flurry of alarm race through her like a jolt from an electrical wire. She'd been so absorbed in the conversation, she hadn't noticed that he'd somehow managed to move down the length of the sofa to her corner of it.

"I know lots of people. And *they* all know lots of people. And . . ."

"Is one of them blackmailing Jenkins?" he asked softly. The fact that his voice was so low and she could hear him meant he was entirely too close. She eased away from him, farther into the corner, though there wasn't much room for retreat.

"Grady, I . . ."

He seemed to sense that Hilary's withdrawal wasn't just a matter of physical distance and changed the subject to the more neutral topic of her studies. In the middle of her explanation of the poetry they were reading in her Romanticism seminar, Charlie called out as he came in the atrium door with her bags.

When Grady yelled back that they were in the family room, the vibration of his chest against her back made Hilary aware that she was leaning back against Grady, while his arm was still casually slung around her. He was even closer to her now than he'd been before. Worse still, she had become quite comfortable there, feeling the warmth and protection of his arm.

She couldn't let this happen—not again. She reminded herself why she didn't need involvement with anyone, particularly not with a man like Grady. Abruptly, she stiffened under his arm and scooted away. "I have to go grade exams." Scrambling off the sectional, Hilary fled for the guest room upstairs.

AFTER SHE HEARD both Grady and Stacy go to bed, she went back to the family room to get some serious work done. As an undergrad, she'd learned that she worked best between eleven and two at night. Setting up her laptop computer on the cocktail table, she sat cross-legged on the couch and wrote, working first on her paper for the Romanticism seminar and then on her dissertation on Decadence in the late nineteenth century. After going through a few more exam papers, she curled up in one corner of the sectional with a book so she could read and relax for a while before she went to bed. The quiet of the house was broken by the soft beep of her pager.

She snapped upright at the sound. Damn. Who on earth could it be at almost two-thirty in the morning? *Only one way to find out*, she thought as she tiptoed into the kitchen, picked up the telephone, and dialed the service she'd subscribed to when she had begun her hostessing business.

The woman on the other end of the line was friendly. Most likely, at this hour, she hadn't talked to anyone for a while and was starting to get lonely. Additionally, as Hilary recalled from having spoken with her before, Judy seemed to live vicariously through the hectic lives of the people whose messages she took. She always sounded entirely too cheerful about the various crises that were a hallmark of the life of Number 537.

This time was a doozy, and Judy sounded as if she was in her glory. It was one of Hilary's many friends, Zeke Murdough. He'd been arrested—again—and he'd somehow managed to convince the police that his one telephone call was going to have to be to a paging service. They were going to allow him to take the return call.

Rapidly she dialed the number, wondering what trouble he'd gotten himself into this time. Fortunately, it had always been something minor in the past. Despite their knowledge of his activities and their desire to catch him for something serious, Zeke had always been wily—or lucky—enough to avoid capture for anything major.

"Zeke Murdough, please," she told the answering operator. "He had me paged."

"He's waiting right here for your call. Just a moment."

"Ree?" Zeke's deep voice came through the line.

"What have you gotten yourself into this time?" she hissed, praying that this wasn't the big one.

"Just cool your jets, kiddo. I got in a fight at Lou's."

"Lou's? That takes real talent." Lou's was a bar in chic Shadyside. She'd been going there regularly for five years and she'd never seen a fight there yet.

"Can you come and get me?" He sounded pitiful, and she reminded herself that she was talking to a man who was big enough and tough enough to make Teamsters and Hell's Angels nervous.

"At this hour? Are you nuts? And anyway..." She wasn't sure exactly how to explain what the problem was. She knew Grady would have a fit if she went to get Zeke by herself, and she didn't want to go and wake him.

"Hilary? Is something wrong?"

She whirled around in response to the voice behind her. It was Grady, wearing only a pair of jeans. She gaped at the bare chest covered with a mat of curly dark hair and felt goose bumps rise on her legs . . . and elsewhere.

"Ree?"

"Hilary?"

She shook her head in an effort to collect herself. "Just a second, Zeke," she said into the receiver before looking up at Grady guiltily. "It's my friend. He wants me to come and bail him out of jail."

"Jail?" Grady's voice rose a full octave.

She shrugged helplessly. "He was in a fight."

"Isn't there anyone else he can call?"

"I'm his one phone call. He had to beg for them to let him page me and have me call back."

"Ree?" The voice carried over the line.

Grady sighed. It sounded as if he were taking the burdens of the world on his shoulders. "Tell him we'll come and get him."

"Are you sure?"

"Don't test me on this one."

"Thanks, Grady." She spoke into the receiver again. "Zeke, we'll be there as soon as we can. Should I call Stephen?"

"Maybe you'd better. He came last time, though. Weren't you engaged to any other lawyers?"

"Just the one, Zeke. See you soon."

"Thanks, Ree. You're a doll."

"Don't forget it." She replaced the receiver on the hook.

"Hilary, please tell me that wasn't Zeke Murdough."

"Do you want me to tell the truth or do you want me to make you feel better?" *She* wanted to curl her fingers in the hair on his chest.

"Never mind. You just answered my question. I can't believe you know that guy. Our department's been trying to nab him for months."

In an effort not to stare at his bare chest, she fixed her gaze on his face. It didn't help. His hair was sleep rumpled and she kept imagining what it would feel like against her skin. Obviously, her common sense had gone to sleep a couple of hours ago.

"Come on, let's go. Unless we're going to let Zeke sit there all night."

"I have to make one phone call first." She reached for the receiver again.

"Just hurry."

Hilary dialed the number and was relieved when it was picked up on the third ring. "Hello?" The voice sounded sleepy, but then, she had known it would.

"Stephen, it's Ree."

"Ree? What time is it?"

"Two-thirty."

"In the morning?" He groaned. "Who is it this time?"

"Zeke."

"Not again . . ."

"Again. Main Booking?"

"I'll be there. Why, I don't know." There was silence for an instant. "Hey, Ree?"

"Yes?"

"Can you make the next one another lawyer? It'd be nice if you had someone else you could call in the dead of night."

"I'll see what I can do, Stephen. See you in a bit."

# 4

WHEN THEY WERE SETTLED in the Mazda and on their way to the downtown station, Grady finally asked the question that had been nagging at him since the moment he'd heard who was on the phone. "How do you know Zeke Murdough?"

"He lived downstairs from me when I had an apartment in South Oakland during my first year of grad school."

While South Oakland bordered on—and in some places overlapped—the worst of the city's slums, its proximity to the university and, more important, its cheapness had turned entire blocks of otherwise-unrentable tenements into prime student housing. Since Hilary was a student, it made perfect sense that she'd lived there at some stage, just as it made sense that Zeke Murdough had lived in the same building. What *didn't* make sense was that they'd somehow become friends during that time.

"We used to take him with us when we went to the grocery store," she added.

"Oh." Well, that explained everything. Apparently, she thought it did, anyway.

"My roommates and I—the ones I had then, before Michael and Paul—were always running to the supermarket at three in the morning, and Zeke was the logical choice to take with us. He was usually awake, and no mugger, rapist or murderer with any common sense or preservational instinct would take on someone his size. How would they know he's really about as dangerous as an oversize teddy bear?"

Actually, it did explain a lot, though thinking of Zeke Murdough as a protector, even only an ostensible one, was a contradiction in terms, at least in his mind. "Hilary, you... Do you know he's a smuggler?"

"Suspected, never convicted," she corrected solemnly, as if the distinction mattered. "And, anyway, it's just cigarettes and liquor. Who's he hurting besides the tax man? To say nothing about the fact that he brings in all kinds of wine and liquor the stores don't even carry."

"Hilary, I'm not exactly in a humor to debate liquor stores with you right now." The proposal to turn them over to private enterprise and get the state out of the liquor business had been a hot issue in Pennsylvania for years. As far as Grady was concerned, Hilary's relationship with Zeke Murdough and her safety were both far more important than whether or not the man was doing a public service. "Does he always call you to bail him out?"

"Zeke is my friend. We've been friends for five years. Who else can you call to bail you out besides your friends?"

"Zeke is dangerous, honey."

Hilary was nearly as shocked at the endearment as she was at her own reaction to it. Her head snapped sharply in his direction, her heart began to thud rapidly, and she felt an alarming shortness of breath. She tried to ignore them both, but it didn't work, and she was grateful for the huge shirt that concealed all the signs that he was getting to her.

"Zeke would never hurt me," she said.

"Not intentionally, maybe. But what if you're there some day when he gets arrested with booze? They'll haul you in, too, and they won't believe you don't know anything. You haven't been along on buys, have you?"

She didn't answer him, which was an answer in itself.

"Do you really think that when the police or the LCB or the ATF comes in, they're going to be able to sort out the innocent bystanders?"

"Grady, I have managed to take care of myself for twenty-six years without your assistance or advice," she said sharply.

He choked. "You don't mean you're involved, do you?"

"Not that it's any of your business, but no, I'm not." She didn't know why she bothered to tell him that—she might as well let him think the worst, and be done with it. Lord knew nothing else she'd said or done had discouraged his interest in her, and the only thing left was shock treatment. "You can ask Zeke."

"But you were there." His voice was anguished.

"They're my friends."

Grady shut up, leaned back in the seat, and closed his eyes.

"YOU MUST BE THE LATEST victim." The man with the sandy-blond hair, who was already at the police station when Grady and Hilary arrived, didn't even say hello to Hilary before he made the cryptic comment to Grady. Impossibly, at three o'clock in the morning, he was wearing a suit and tie that made him appear as if he were on his way to shoot a *GQ* ad. "I'm Stephen. Don't bother with a last name. It'll just confuse you, and more confusion is the last thing you need. You have my sympathies."

"What? Victim?" Grady felt as if he'd stepped through the looking glass and met the world's best-dressed Mad Hatter.

Stephen laughed again, and Hilary scowled at him. "Leave him alone, Stephen. This is Grady Thompson, the police detective that's investigating Ryan's case."

"Wrong, Ree. I recognize that look. I invented it, remember?"

"Stephen . . ." The tone of her voice definitely implied warning. So did the look in her eyes. If the daggers she was shooting at him had been real, he would have been crucified on the far wall.

"Okay, Ree, I'll drop it . . . for now. I have everything taken care of. As soon as you give them the bail, we can take Zeke. I'm advising him to plead self-defense. For once, thank God, the other guy seems to have taken the first swing, and there are a lot of witnesses."

Hilary's pager sounded again, and she groaned in disgust. "What could it be now? Here, Stephen," she said, handing him the money before she headed off to the pay phone.

When Hilary returned a few moments later, Zeke rushed at her as if he thought she had saved his life, swung her up in his huge arms, and thanked her profusely. In return, she cracked him smartly on the side of the head, an action that made him put her down immediately, though he still held her by the shoulders and kept on thanking her.

"You idiot! How many times have I bailed you out in the last two months?"

"My mother thanks you, my father thanks you, my dog—"

"Shut up, Zeke! Enough is enough! Next time, you can sit here and rot! Do you hear me?"

"I've seen this routine twenty times," Stephen told Grady softly, with a bemused shake of his head. "I still can't get over it, though. They look like Mutt and Jeff, don't they?"

"It happens often?"

"Every time. Get used to it."

*Used to it?* If he lived to be a hundred, he'd never get used to this insanity. She was so cute when she was mad, though—like a kitten fearlessly taking on a full-grown mountain gorilla.

Hilary's tirade was short-lived, interrupted when she suddenly remembered the telephone call she'd gone to answer. "We have to go and get Manny."

"What's he done this time?" Stephen wailed.

"Who's Manny?" Grady asked.

"Michael's brother," explained Zeke.

"Then why doesn't Michael get him?" Grady demanded. "Who *is* Michael, anyway?"

"Michael's my other housemate. You met him the other afternoon, but you probably don't remember."

Grady remembered. The Hercules clone that had called him a pervert and then laughed at him just before he'd gone around the bend.

"Paul can't find Michael. We don't know Christie's last name," Hilary continued. "And Paul doesn't have a car. He left it with Marshall so we could have the furniture."

"Who's Marshall?" Grady asked, thoroughly confused.

"Paul's ex-lover," Stephen said in an aside to Grady. Turning back to Hilary, he asked, "Where is he?"

"He who?"

"Manny Cassimatis."

"Wheeling."

"Wheeling?" Grady's head whirled as he assimilated the information and was hit by its full impact. "That's in West Virginia! It's fifty miles away!"

A HALF HOUR LATER, Grady drove the Mazda through the state game preserve while Hilary dozed in the passenger seat beside him. He grumbled to himself, wondering why

on earth he was on his way to Wheeling at three-thirty in
the morning to get someone he'd never seen out of jail. If
he'd had any sense at all, he would have told her to tell
Manny to sit in Wheeling until they located Michael—
however long it took. He couldn't, though. Those big blue
eyes had gotten to him, and he knew he would have volunteered to drive to Alaska if she'd asked him.

Grady stole glances at Hilary as often as he could during the drive. She looked so fragile and delicate when she
was sleeping. Her hair tumbled around her shoulders, reflecting the glow from the dash, and her lips were parted
as if in invitation to a kiss. She looked so peaceful, he decided he could get used to watching her sleep. He remembered vividly what her body felt like underneath those
voluminous men's clothes—alternately soft and firm in all
the right places—and he had to shift uneasily in the seat
to ease the sudden pressure that was building again inside
his jeans. He felt like a silly teenager, but he couldn't help
it; whenever he looked at Hilary, he got aroused.

They were almost into Wheeling when Hilary awoke,
stretching like a cat to work out the stiffness that had set
in from sleeping in the car seat. Observing her, Grady
couldn't help thinking about what it would be like to
watch her awaken on a regular basis. It was a thought that
warmed him deep inside.

"The police station's just ahead on the right," she said
sleepily.

"How do you know where the Wheeling police station
is?"

She shrugged. "I came down here once to get Zeke."

He was relatively sure he didn't want to know for what.

When they walked into the station, Grady saw a young
man who looked like a twenty-year-old Hercules, and he
knew it was Manny even before Hilary stormed up to him,

smacked him on the side of the head—just as she had Zeke—and glared at both him and the pair of young men who flanked him on the bench. "Do you mean to tell me the three of you don't have enough between you for a crummy fifty-dollar fine?"

"Ree!" Manny wailed. It was as obvious that he'd been the recipient of her anger before as it had been with Zeke.

"And you . . . For heaven's sake, Manny! A police-woman! Don't you have any sense at all?"

"I didn't know she was a cop!"

"What are you doing, trying to pick up hookers in a cheap bar like that, anyway?"

"Ree!"

"Just you wait until Michael hears about this! He's gonna wring your neck!" With that, she spun on her heel and stomped over to the desk.

"You must be the latest victim," Manny said to Grady, as calmly and cheerfully as if Hilary had never hit or yelled at him.

*Victim?* Was it supposed to mean something? "I'm Grady Thompson."

"The pervert?"

Had everybody in Pittsburgh heard about that?

"Manny, just shut up!" Hilary snapped over her shoulder, as the word carried to her clear across the room. "I don't want to hear another word from you except 'Thank you,' and, 'Goodbye.'"

"Yes, Ree," he answered sheepishly. The two next to him snickered. "Thank you."

Laughter threatened as Grady considered how effortlessly Hilary handled not only Zeke, but Manny and his friends, as well. He'd give anything to see her with students; she was probably the tiny terror of the English department.

When she walked back to join the four of them, she yawned and rubbed her eyes wearily. "Come on, Grady. Let's go home."

"See, I told you!" Manny insisted with an unrepentant grin. "He is—"

Hilary clenched her jaw as she glared at him. "Manny, you have a mind like—"

"A steel trap?" he offered.

"Not exactly. Goodbye, Manny. I don't want to hear from you again until you're housebroken." Pivoting on her heel, she strode from the police station, Grady following in her wake.

"Hilary, you want me to drive back? You look exhausted." He halted her protest with one raised hand. "Don't forget, I had three hours' sleep before all this started."

"All right, then. I don't think I'll argue with you."

"It wouldn't do you any good, anyway. You're too tired to drive." He slipped his arm companionably around her waist as they walked to the car, opened the door for her, and helped her inside. She accepted his assistance with such sweet grace and uncharacteristic docility, he thought briefly about kissing her, but decided it would be pushing his luck.

Hilary sleepily stretched out her legs in front of her seat and looked up at Grady. He'd been an awfully good sport about everything that had happened that night, and he'd been so cute when he'd yelled, "West Virginia?" and turned all red. It was almost a shame that she couldn't get involved with him.

Turning her head away from him and curling up on the seat, she fell asleep.

When they got back to Grady's house, Hilary was still sound asleep and Grady decided to carry her into the house. Circling the car again, he opened the passenger door and scooped her into his arms. It surprised him, somehow, but she didn't weigh anything when she wasn't resisting him. She was so tiny and seemed so fragile, it was difficult for him to imagine that she could struggle as fiercely as he remembered. As he juggled her to open the atrium door, he hoped it wouldn't wake her—but then, maybe he *didn't* hope for that.

"Grady?"

"Hmm?"

"What are you doing?"

"Carrying you."

"Carrying me where?"

"Into the kitchen. We're home."

Hilary didn't like the sound of that—not at all. The way Grady said it, he made it seem as if it was *their* house, not *his*. "Grady, put me down this minute."

"Okay." He was being too agreeable, and Hilary knew the reason for it immediately when she found herself seated on the edge of the kitchen countertop. Grady blocked any possible escape route as he stood in front of her, his hands resting on either side of her on the counter. As far as she was concerned, he was entirely too close for comfort.

"Grady, no!" she hissed.

"Look, Hilary, it's late," he began, sounding stern. "I've had an . . . interesting couple of days here. First, I find out that the woman who made me wreck a vintage T-Bird and thoroughly humiliate myself appears to be the mistress of a pro football player but isn't, although she is an important link in a blackmail case. All right, I can accept that. I can accept that you don't seem to know any women. I can accept that you have an exceedingly peculiar selection of friends. Why, I can't begin to guess. Maybe I'm a glutton for punishment, but I'm still interested. You seemed to be, too, once you realized I wasn't really a pervert. But every time I try to get within ten feet of you, you scurry away from me as if I were a plague carrier. For God's sake, Hilary, I've been in three states and two police stations since two-thirty this morning. Two people I have never laid eyes on before tonight have referred to me as 'the latest victim.' I'm starting to feel like one, and I have no intention of letting you go anywhere until I get some sort of explanation that makes sense!"

Hilary closed her eyes and leaned her head back against the doors of the cabinets. "Grady, it's five-thirty in the morning! Can we talk about this later?"

"Would you like a drink or coffee?"

"No."

"It was a choice, not a yes-or-no question. *Which* would you like?"

She sighed, resigned to the fact that he wasn't going to give in and let her go back to sleep without having this discussion, and then mumbled, "Coffee."

"Is instant all right?"

"Fine."

Hilary made one aborted attempt at flight while Grady was boiling water. She didn't get three steps before she was back on the counter again. Finally, once the coffee was made, he placed a mug in her hand, steered her into the family room by the nape of her neck, parked her on the sectional, and sat down beside her.

"You're angry," she observed glumly, staring into the steam rising from the mug.

"No, just confused."

"Where would you like me to start?"

"God only knows...."

"You can't get interested in me, Grady."

"Too late. I already am."

"You *can't.* I'll only mess up your life, and I can't deal with the guilt of another one."

"Another victim?"

She nodded, but didn't speak.

"What are they talking about?"

"The ex-fiancés . . ."

"Fiancés? As in plural?"

"Plural, as in seven."

*"Seven?"* His voice rose a full octave.

She nodded again.

"Why do you think I'll be another victim?"

"It must be apparent I'm not the only one who thinks so."

"But why?"

"Grady, I'm not a good risk—"

"Why don't you let me be the judge of that?"

She groaned wearily, closing her eyes as she leaned back against the sofa. "That's it, precisely. That's *exactly* what they all said."

"And?" he prompted.

"And I'm not married to any of them, am I?" she demanded tartly. "Obviously, they were wrong."

"What happened, Hilary?"

"Which time?"

"You don't need to give me all the gory details, but there *must* be a common thread."

"I made them all miserable and crazy." She paused. "Grady, I don't want to hurt you."

He gathered her into his arms and, too exhausted to fight him, she let her head drop to rest against his shoulder. It felt good, safe, secure being there, so close she could both feel and hear his heart beat.

"Is that why you said you wouldn't go out with me?" he asked softly.

She nodded, and he moved his hand up to the back of her head, stroking the soft silk of her hair until he felt her nuzzle against him in response.

"Oh, Hilary..." His arms tightened around her.

"Grady, you can't let yourself care about me."

"Too late, honey," he told her. "I already do."

She pulled away from him. "Listen to me! Read my lips, for God's sake! I'm a full-time student who's also juggling a couple of very demanding part-time jobs. I don't keep regular hours—for heaven's sake, I was still awake when the page came at two-thirty in the morning. You'd been asleep for hours."

"That doesn't matter—"

"Yes, it does, Grady. Don't you see? You need order in your life, not some flake that goes flying off—"

"Hilary, *none* of that matters."

"It *does* matter, Grady! Go find yourself some nice, sensible woman with a station wagon and support hose—"

"I don't want a sensible woman, dammit! Hilary, I want you!" Grady lowered his mouth to hers, blocking any further protests she might make.

As their lips met, Hilary knew her arguments hadn't made the slightest impression on either of them. And it was only a matter of seconds before she forgot why she'd been arguing at all and parted her lips to admit the gentle probing of Grady's tongue. As he explored the deepest recesses of her mouth in a steadily more insistent manner, a warm feeling spread throughout her body and she returned his kiss wholeheartedly, her tongue moving to parry with his. It felt so gloriously right to kiss Grady, to be held in his arms and to hold him, that Hilary scarcely noticed when they stretched out on the sectional by mutual accord, with their bodies pressed eagerly together.

Even before Grady's hand moved to capture her breast, Hilary felt the nipple tingle and stiffen with anticipation. When he touched it, she moaned and arched into his palm, regretting the layers of clothing that separated her skin from his. He cupped the round fullness in his hand, stroking the hard peak until it throbbed with desire—a pulse that echoed deep in her lower body. Her every breath was a struggle for air, a sharp gasp that ended in a sigh.

Grady pressed himself to her thigh, making the evidence of his powerful arousal apparent to her—evidence that grew stronger as she writhed against him, in turn increasing her own heated reaction. Burying his face in the side of her throat, he nuzzled and licked the soft skin behind her ear. Soft mewls of pleasure escaped Hilary's lips.

He strummed his thumb across her nipple and then smiled when her breath caught in her throat and she shivered again. In a husky whisper, he asked, "Can you imagine what it'll be like when we make love?"

Even if she could have summoned the strength—and the oxygen—to debate his use of the word *when* instead of *if*, she would have been stretching the limits of credibility. She didn't have the slightest doubt that it would happen, and sometime soon. "Uh-uh," she finally forced out.

"You sound as if you're dying," he told her, sliding his hand down her side. Once he got to her hip, he left his hand there, and he noted that her trembling and ragged breathing continued unabated.

"I'll be fine," she lied, her voice raw with unfulfilled desire. Her eyelids were squeezed so tightly shut, she could feel tears at the corners of her eyes. She struggled to get herself under control, but she'd been so close—for that matter, she still was.

"I can help," he offered gallantly, his hand moving across her thigh in a direction that left no question about what type of assistance he had in mind.

With astonishing speed and strength, her hand closed over his, stopping him before it could advance another inch. "No, Grady."

"Are you sure?"

After pausing to take a deep breath and swallow heavily, she said, in a remarkably stalwart voice, "I'm sure."

With a resigned sigh, Grady gathered Hilary in his arms, nestling her back against his chest. He pressed a soft kiss to the top of her head that prompted another momentary bout of trembling. Then he whispered, "It's been a long night, and it's late. Go to sleep."

"Good night, Grady," she whispered back, still struggling with the clamorous demands of her body and assuring herself that she was, indeed, going to live to laugh about this someday.

"Good night, honey."

Somehow, the endearment—and the position—felt right.


"DADDY?"

Grady groaned and tried to sit up, but his freedom was hampered by the arm that was still pinned beneath Hilary. Easing it out and wincing as the sudden rush of blood into it made it tingle, he opened one eye to peer at his daughter. "Huh?"

"Why are you and Hilary sleeping on the sofa?"

The girl was obviously far too sharp. Hoping to change the subject before she asked any more awkward questions, he asked, "What time is it?" His voice sounded hoarse, unused.

"Quarter to seven."

The other eye opened. Sort of. He blinked several times, verifying that it still worked.

"You're usually up by now," accused Stacy.

"I don't usually drive to Wheeling at three o'clock in the morning," he growled, running the hand that had feeling over his face as if to assure himself it was still there.

"West Virginia?"

"Yep." He crawled over Hilary to get off the sofa. She didn't move a muscle. How could anyone sleep with a conversation going on over her head?

"Why?"

"You ask too many questions."

"You both have all your clothes on," Stacy observed.

"You also notice entirely too much. Don't you have to go to school?"

"Not yet, Daddy!" She went into the kitchen and Grady trailed after her. He immediately regretted not heading for some other part of the house, as she ruthlessly continued the interrogation. "Is Hilary the one that made you wreck the car?"

"Where'd you hear that?"

"Charlie."

"Maybe he'd like to adopt you." He began to make coffee—real coffee this time, not instant. He could already tell he was going to need every last milligram of caffeine he could get into his system.

"At least Charlie and Jenny *have* a car."

"You don't drive yet. Why do you care if we have a car?"

"It'll only be three months and twelve days until I'm old enough to drive."

Grady groaned. "Don't remind me. And anyway, I think we'll have the T-Bird back by then. Hey, wait a minute. We have another car."

She made a face that expressed her opinion of the plainclothes police car and returned to the original subject. He wondered where this persistent streak might have come from; she certainly hadn't inherited it from him. "What were you and Hilary doing in West Virginia?"

"None of your business."

Stacy's eyes widened. "Did you and Hilary get married?"

"No. And it's Maryland that you don't have to wait— Forget I said that. I don't want to give you any ideas."

"What's the age limit in Maryland?"

"I don't know, but if you want to live to be old enough to drive, you'll drop it."

"Do you have a hangover? You're sure grouchy."

"No. I'm just operating on three and a half hours of sleep."

"What time did you get back?"

"Five-thirty."

"And then you and Hilary went to sleep together."

"If you *ever* repeat that, I'm gonna sell you to the gypsies."

"But why do you have all your clothes on?"

"Are you back to that again? Where do you learn these things?"

"We have sex ed at school. Besides, I *am* almost sixteen." Her voice was rife with grown-up affront.

"I'm gonna look for a convent school."

"I thought you were giving me to the gypsies."

"Don't push your luck. Are you sure you're fifteen?"

The conversation was mercifully interrupted by Charlie's arrival at the atrium door. It was still locked, so he had to knock. When Grady came to open it, Charlie peered at him curiously before following him back to the kitchen. "You look like hell."

"Thanks. You're not the first one to make that observation this morning." He picked up a mug and eyed the coffeemaker, not certain he could wait until it finished dripping.

"How much sleep did you get?"

With a surprising degree of dexterity, he slid the pot out from under the basket, replacing it with the mug so the coffee could drain straight into it. "Eleven to two and six to six-thirty."

"Why, for God's sake?"

"I don't want to discuss it." He started to pull out the filled mug, but before he could put the pot back into place, Charlie slid in another mug for himself.

"Fine. How's Hilary?"

"Still sleeping."

"Hilary and Daddy slept together," Stacy chirped, in a voice that was entirely too innocent to be real. She knew exactly what she was saying, and Grady knew she knew it.

"What?"

"On the sofa. Fully clothed. For half an hour," Grady added, glaring at his daughter. She was going to the gypsies as soon as he could find some. "Stacy, go find someone else to torture. I haven't had enough sleep to deal with this."

"Have you had enough sleep to deal with the Connors hearing?" Charlie asked.

"They moved it up? To today?" Grady wanted nothing more than to crawl into a hole and pull it in after him. He wanted to sleep for the next year. He didn't want to go and testify against anybody today.

"Lieutenant Angelucci sent me over to baby-sit our favorite—and only—lead in the Ryan Jenkins case while you're gone. The note didn't pan out; Forensics said it's printed on standard copy paper with the most common inkjet printer in North America, and the only finger-prints on it are Hilary's roommate's. By the way, they want you down at the courthouse at nine o'clock."

"Maybe a shower'll help." *And another pot of coffee*, he added silently.

"It can't hurt. You really *do* look like hell, you know."

THE HEARING WAS EVERY bit as tedious as Grady had ex-pected it would be. The prosecutors had told him to be there at nine o'clock, they didn't get started until ten, and he didn't get to testify against Connors, who had been implicated in a series of drive-by shootings, until after lunch. As if enough hadn't gone wrong already, he fell asleep on the hard wooden bench in the hall outside the courtroom, and Captain Rogers caught him.

He was relieved to get back to the house again. Maybe he could get a couple of hours' sleep, lying down instead of sitting up, before dinner. He hoped Stacy hadn't hauled in half a dozen friends to listen to the stereo or something equally noisy. Even though he loved her, he had to admit he was relieved to see her coming through the atrium door as he got out of the car.

"Hi, Daddy." She smiled as she reached up to press a kiss to his cheek. "Boy, are you in for a treat!"

She looked entirely too cheerful, and Grady eyed her suspiciously. "What do you mean?"

An impish grin defied all her attempts to suppress it. "Hilary's cooking dinner."

"Why's that so funny?"

"I'm eating at Julie's."

"Will they adopt you? I can't find any gypsies."

"Then you won't have anybody who knows how to cook," she answered ominously.

"That bad?"

"Worse. I think Charlie's gonna hurt himself."

"Why?"

"He's trying not to laugh. Bye, Daddy. Good luck."

Grady watched after Stacy as she crossed the lawns to her friend's house. Somehow, he felt like a captain whose crew had just deserted him. Worse, he had a feeling that there was a damn good reason for abandonment of the ship.

His worst fears were confirmed when he walked through the patio door and found Charlie sitting on one of the stools at the breakfast bar, watching the activity in the kitchen with a look that hovered between fascination and horror. Grady had seen that look before—on gawkers at car accidents. It didn't bode well for dinner.

"Show's over, Charlie. Time to go home."

"Do I have to? This is better than watching Jenny cook."

"Sorry, Charlie. Spectators are not generally welcome at disasters."

"You've talked to Stacy."

"If you're asking if she's warned me, yes, she has."

"Do you have lots of bicarb? I wish I owned stock."

The subject of their speculation was blissfully unaware of their dire predictions. She was too busy listening to the person on the other end of the telephone—obviously Paul—trying to talk her through dinner preparations. "Shouldn't we have started with something easier?" she was asking him.

The appearance of the kitchen, and of Hilary, suggested that she needed a lot more help than a mere phone conversation could provide. There was flour everywhere. Some of the pans and dishes piled on either side of the sink hadn't been used in so long that Grady didn't recognize them as his own. The pan in which the meat cooked must have exploded, since there was a grease stain that started on one side of the ceiling, crossed it completely, and trailed down the wall on the other side. Another pot that looked big enough to cook lobsters for the twelfth fleet boiled vigorously, turning the kitchen into a sauna. A bag of noodles that had put up a vigorous struggle had lost and its contents were spilled out across the counter and onto the floor. Grady decided on the spot that he didn't ever want to see Hilary make a complicated meal, like a roast or fried chicken. Forget cordon bleu.

In the center of the mess stood Hilary, blithely ignorant of her surroundings, barefoot, in a voluminous man's bowling shirt that hung to mid-thigh. He wondered, idly, if there was a pair of shorts beneath. Her hair was piled in a heap on the top of her head and held by something that looked remarkably like a purple sweat sock. When Grady studied it more closely, he realized that was exactly what it was. Despite the fact that she was crunching through uncooked noodles at every turn, despite the flour that coated almost every inch of her, despite the fact that his kitchen looked like he should apply for federal disaster aid, Grady thought she looked absolutely adorable. He smiled and shook his head.

"You wouldn't look so pleased if you'd been here when she baked the cakes this afternoon."

"Cakes?"

"The first went down the garbage disposal, unbaked, the second went out to the neighbors' dogs, and they buried it, and the third one is still in a state of limbo."

"It's what?"

"She won't frost it until somebody in authority—you, I think—decides it might be edible. She asked Stacy and me, but we both like you too much to make a decision like that for you."

"It looks that bad?"

"Remember when Mount St. Helen erupted?"

"Oh."

"She's been on the phone with Paul most of the afternoon."

Grady sighed. "Does it look promising?"

"I called the plumber before the last call to Paul. He should be here shortly."

"Plumber?"

"No one told her you can't drain the meat into the sink."

"It's clogged?"

"Not yet, but I think he should look at it when he takes the towel out of the garbage disposal."

"What?"

"It wouldn't have been so bad if she hadn't turned it on."

Grady cringed.

"It sucked that silverware right in there after it."

"You're enjoying this," Grady accused.

"Hell, yes. It isn't my kitchen." Charlie paused dramatically. "Other than that, things have been pretty calm since the firemen left."

"Firemen?"

"It really was just a little grease fire and the neighbors had no reason to get excited."

"Oh, God . . ." Grady groaned and closed his eyes.

Soon the plumber arrived, frowned, shook his head at the garbage disposal, and announced, in a voice that was entirely too cheerful to suit Grady, that the Thompsons definitely needed a new unit. A wide-eyed Hilary watched him at work, asking questions and listening to the answers, handing him tools as he needed them. After he was finished, an amazed Grady paid a bill that was sixty percent of the estimate and made a mental note to himself that

he wanted Hilary around when he got the new roof he
needed.

Dinner was marginally better than Grady had expected, if only because he'd expected so little. It was edible, at least. Which was saying something, because the
cake sure wasn't. It looked like corrugated steel and
weighed almost as much. As tactfully as possible, Grady
vetoed wasting frosting on the thing and tried to give it to
the squirrels that lived in the maple tree in the backyard.
They sniffed at it curiously, probably wondering what it
was, then decided they didn't want it any more than the
neighbors' dogs had.

Once they'd settled into the living room after the meal,
Grady turned to Hilary. "We have to talk."

# 5

HILARY AND GRADY were curled up on the sectional with their coffee.

"I know we have to talk," she answered softly, looking down into the mug she turned nervously between her hands.

Grady reached to stop the fidgeting movement and assured her, "Don't look so nervous about it, honey. If I haven't yelled yet, I'm not likely to start now."

"I'll pay for the plumber."

"Don't worry about the plumber."

"I'll pay to have the ceiling fixed."

"Don't worry about the ceiling, either."

"I'll pay to have the driveway resurfaced."

"Don't worry about— What happened to the driveway?" His jaw clenched suddenly, entirely against his will, and there was nothing he could do to stop it before she saw it.

"The seal on the oil pan decided it didn't want to be part of the Mazda anymore," she confessed sorrowfully.

"Oh. Don't worry about it." He shrugged and smiled with at least some semblance of sincerity. After the job she'd done on the kitchen, he'd expected far worse. "So there's an oil stain in the driveway. I'll learn to live with it."

"It ran off. It'll kill the grass and flowers."

"I'll get more grass and flowers."

"I'll pay for them."

She looked so pitiful, with those big blue eyes, that Grady couldn't have gotten angry at her, even if she told him she'd killed the sugar maples, too. He wanted to gather her in his arms and tell her it didn't matter and convince her he meant it. "You don't have to do that, Hilary. It's not important—"

"This, from a man who had his lawn landscaped and sodded? Really, Grady—"

"What makes you think I had my lawn landscaped and sodded?"

"I'd bet my last penny you couldn't find a dandelion in that whole yard."

Hilary was right, but for some peculiar reason Grady didn't want to admit it. She made it sound like a personal deficiency.

"Or crabgrass."

"The neighbors wouldn't stand for it. They'd make me move."

She shook one slim finger in front of his nose and he grappled with the urge to catch it in his lips. "That grass has a name, doesn't it?"

"Of course—Lester," Grady replied with an engaging smile.

"Grady..." she moaned. "I mean it's some sort of fancy grass, a particular breed."

"It's only grass."

"We paved our yard." Hilary said each word deliberately, as if it ought to make a point to him.

Grady considered the statement for a moment and burst out laughing. "You did what?"

"When we bought the firehouse, we decided to request a volunteer for lawn duty. Everyone took one step back and we voted unanimously to buy slate and cover the whole thing so we wouldn't have to deal with it."

"You own that firehouse? I assumed you rented it."

"That much space? Grady, really… Any landlord worth his salt would have converted that building into at least four apartments."

Now that he thought about it, she was right. His house was big, but he could have dropped two of it into the firehouse, with room to spare. "Which one of you owns it?"

"All three of us do. Me, Michael, and Paul."

"Wait a minute— The three of you had enough money to pay for that building and do the renovation outright?"

"Of course not. We went to the bank and got a mortgage, just like everybody else."

"No banker in his right mind gives a mortgage to three unrelated people to convert a firehouse." *Particularly not those three,* Grady added silently. He astutely kept that observation to himself.

"Alex did."

"Who's Alex? And does he still work for that bank?"

"Alex was after Stephen."

*Another fiancé,* Grady deduced. "He knows you, and he still lent you money?"

"I *am* financially responsible." She looked offended by the implication that she wasn't. "Besides, I threatened him."

"With what? You were gonna bake him a cake?" Immediately, Grady winced. He shouldn't have said that.

Hilary ignored the insult. "Actually, I threatened to move in with him again if he didn't lend us the money to buy the firehouse."

"And?"

"And Alex not only approved the loan, he cosigned it. Then he told Paul and Michael that if they could live with me, they deserved a medal. I don't think he's ever forgiven me for that little problem with his oven."

"His oven?"

"I tried making Alex's mother's hot-cross-buns recipe."

"And?"

"I didn't know that the little *t* meant teaspoon, not tablespoon, so I put in too much salt."

Grady wasn't sure he wanted to know, but he had to ask. Not knowing was like waiting for the other shoe to drop. "But what does that have to do with the oven?"

"The recipe said to put it someplace warm to rise, so I stuck the Tupperware bowl in the oven."

"Tupperware? In the oven?"

"Only the pilot light was on, so I didn't think it would get too hot."

Obviously, she'd been wrong. "Total damages?"

"Whole new oven liner and that round thing on the bottom that burns." She paused for a moment and sighed. "And a Tupperware bowl."

"Makes the garbage disposal sound like nothing." Grady was simultaneously envious of, sorry for, and angry at the unknown Alex, the second "victim."

"That's what Alex thought. He yelled and I moved out."

"How long did you live together?"

"Ten days."

"Is that why you're so afraid of getting involved with me, Hilary?" Grady asked gently.

She shook her head. "I'm not afraid, Grady. I'm concerned for you. I like you, and I don't want to hurt you."

He reached out to stroke her cheek, stilling the motion of her head. She pressed her cheek into his cupped palm. "Don't you think I'm old enough to take care of myself?"

"That's what—"

"—they all said," he finished, recalling what she'd told him the night before. "Don't lump me in with them, honey."

"Grady, you're the kind of person whose address book is alphabetized by last name—"

"Hilary, don't start—"

"—with notations of birthdays and Christmas cards—"

"—this again—"

"And I'm a flake whose address book is—"

"Hilary—"

"—a shoe box filled with matchbooks and old envelopes and scraps of—"

Grady stopped her the only way he knew would work. He slid both arms around her waist and pulled her toward him as he caught her mouth with his. He only teased her lips for an instant before moving in for the final resolution of their argument, his tongue delving into the sweetness that tasted of beef Stroganoff and wine and Hilary.

Her head swam with the sensation, consigning the thought of the alphabetized address book to oblivion and replacing it with thoughts of Grady. Why was she arguing with him, anyway?

When she went limp in his arms, Grady eased his mouth away from hers. "That's why I can't walk away from you, honey," he whispered in a voice that was husky with desire and emotion. "I don't give a damn about the garbage disposal or the ceiling or the driveway or the grass—not when I can have this instead."

"But, Grady..." she began, regaining her faculties enough to remember why things couldn't possibly work out between them.

"If you can still argue with me, I didn't kiss you enough."

He proceeded to prove his point, quite successfully. Hilary melted away as her protests did, like the last snow in a soft, warm rain, its mass changing into a raging stream swollen to flood levels. This time, the teasing came at the end, as Grady nibbled lightly at the corner of her lips, pausing to catch the sigh that escaped her.

"And if you start arguing again," he growled huskily, "I'll haul you out into the backyard and prove exactly how much I don't care about the grass."

"The neighbors will be scandalized," Hilary breathed.

"To hell with the neighbors." Grady pushed her back onto the sectional, covering her body with his.

"Grady..." she protested again.

"I'm serious," he warned in a low voice. "Sweetheart..."

Hilary started at the new, more unsettling endearment. This was becoming entirely too serious, and she knew she ought to stop it before she got too used to it. She just didn't know how, or even if she really wanted to anymore.

"...Yes, *sweetheart*," Grady repeated firmly. "You keep saying you don't want to hurt me, Hilary, but you *are* hurting me. I want you more than I've wanted any woman in years—since before Anne died."

"Anne was Stacy's mother—your..." Though it was the first time Grady had mentioned her name, Hilary had seen the evidence of his late wife's past presence in the kitchen and surmised that she'd been the definitive Suzy Homemaker—a conclusion Charlie had confirmed when she'd badgered him into telling her.

"Yes, Hilary. Now shut up...please...and let me talk." His head lowered and his lips touched hers for an instant, as if to seal them. "I've wanted you since before the T-Bird hit the lamppost, and nothing that's happened since then has changed that one bit." Grady ground his hips against hers, making her aware of his arousal. "I've been like this since I met you, honey. Before then, I thought I was dead. I didn't think I was capable of feeling this way ever again." He paused, regaining his composure. "Sweetheart, let me—us—take a chance on this. You say it won't work, but I don't think it's a decision you have any right to make without giving it a chance. We can't *not* try."

"I can't change, Grady! I've tried before!"

"*Don't* change! That's what I'm trying to tell you, you little idiot! I want enough time to prove you can't make me crazy, because what we can have together is stronger than that!"

She moaned and dropped her head back on the sofa, closing her eyes. "No, Grady!"

"*Yes*, Hilary. You feel it, too—don't lie to me! You have to give me a chance, for both of us!"

"But, Grady..."

They were interrupted by the sound of the atrium door opening and then closing again. "Daddy?"

Grady dropped his head and groaned, wishing guiltily that he could get rid of that child for just a few days. She had the most remarkably inconvenient sense of timing. "In here, Stace." He had to get control of himself, and soon. Just then, the telephone rang and he blessed whoever it was that had provided him with a few more very necessary minutes.

"I'll get it!" Thank God she was at the age when every ring of the telephone could generate such boundless enthusiasm. "Hello?" Her breathless answer carried into the family room. "Oh." It obviously wasn't for her.

"Ree?" Stacy had crossed the kitchen and stood in the open doorway of the family room, gaping at the pair on the sectional. "Daddy?"

"Who is it, Stacy?" Grady demanded, his forehead still lowered to Hilary's.

She raised the receiver, stretched on its cord, to her ear, her eyes still on her father and Hilary. "May I ask who's calling?" She lowered the receiver and covered it again with her hand. "It's for Ree. Somebody named Michael."

"Michael?" Hilary squeaked from under Grady, pushing up against his chest. "What on earth could he want?"

Grady rolled off her, drawing himself up so his feet were on the edge of the coffee table, his knees raised, concealing himself. Hilary scrambled to her feet and took the phone from Stacy. "Thanks, Stace. Michael?" She started back into the kitchen, the phone's receiver tucked against her ear.

Stacy came into the family room and sat on the sofa next to Grady. "Daddy? Are you okay?"

He wasn't, not at all. He leaned forward against his thighs, clasping his arms around his knees. "Yes, Stace, I'm fine," he lied.

"Then why do you look like you stepped on a tack?"

The girl was far too bright. He couldn't come up with a reasonable answer for her, and he knew it.

"Daddy?" she asked hesitantly.

"Hmm?"

"I like Ree. A lot. She's nice, even if she can't cook."

"Mm-hmm," Grady agreed, if somewhat noncommittally.

"Maybe you could take her out somewhere—like on a date or something."

"Mm-hmm." He'd been out of circulation entirely too long if his fifteen-year-old was giving him advice.

"If it'd make you more comfortable, maybe you and Hilary and Brandon Pengelly and me could all double-date," she offered.

Grady chuckled to himself at the absurdity of his daughter's suggestion. The way he felt and acted when he was around Hilary, a double date was entirely out of the question. It would give the kids too many ideas. "No, but thanks anyway, kiddo." He laughed again and came to a sudden stop. "Brandon who?"

"Brandon Pengelly."

He peered at her suspiciously. "Who's Brandon Pengelly?"

Stacy's eyes got a dreamy look that Grady recognized all too well, and she chewed her lip nervously. "That's what I came back to ask about. Brandon and Jason Phillips want to double-date with me and Julie on Saturday. Can I?"

"Are there any plans or are you winging it?"

"There's a dance at school. I know you said I couldn't date until I turned sixteen, but it's only three more months and Julie's already sixteen and—"

"Stop." He held up one hand to reinforce his command and prevent any further "ands." "How old are Brandon Pengelly and Jason Phillips?"

"Seventeen." Her eyes begged. "Daddy, please . . ."

He could feel himself weakening, and hesitated just long enough for her to get in another shot.

"It's just a dance and pizza . . . And Julie's mom says I can stay at her house on Saturday night, so if you wanted to take Hilary out, you wouldn't have to worry about getting back in time to meet me."

Grady thought for a moment, closing his eyes because he was afraid she'd see the eagerness the image generated there. "Okay."

The squeal that answered him was so earsplitting, it brought Hilary to the edge of the room, the telephone still in her hand. She laughed as Stacy threw her arms around Grady's neck, thanking him with undisciplined glee. Seeing her there, Stacy attacked Hilary for the telephone and she cut short her conversation with Michael. "Hey, I gotta go. There's somebody here who's gonna murder me if I don't give her the phone. Yeah, well, bye."

Still laughing, Hilary pressed the button to hang up, relinquished the receiver, and gaped after Stacy as she cloistered herself in the closet with the telephone. "Does she do this often?"

Grady shook his head, feeling as if he'd just been run over by a truck. "Not as a rule, but I just gave her permission for her first date."

"Oh. That explains it, then. You look like someone just hit you right between the eyes."

"When did she grow up?"

"Don't ask me. You've been here all along. I'm new here, remember?" She settled in next to him on the sofa. "So what's the story?"

"His name is Brandon...something. Pengelly, that's it. He's seventeen."

"That means he drives."

"I know," Grady answered uneasily. "They're doubling with Julie and Jason something-or-other. To a dance at school and then for a pizza."

"You look like you're gonna throw up."

"The thought *has* crossed my mind."

"Did you give her a curfew?" He gave her an amazed look, and she added, "Well, someone has to be sensible about this. Don't look so surprised that it's me."

"She's going to stay at Julie's afterward, so Julie's mom gets to be the enforcer for both of them." He continued tentatively. "Stacy seems to think it would be nice if we...that is, the two of us...you and me—"

"Have you spoken to Julie's mother?" Hilary interrupted.

"What?" Grady lost his whole train of thought.

"Have you made certain Julie's mother doesn't think they're staying here?"

He considered the possibility. It was sobering. "Oh. No."

"You probably should. That one is the oldest trick in the book, right up there with the one about having car trouble."

"Oh. How do I find out without making an idiot of myself?"

"You get Julie's mom on the phone and—"

"Would you do it?" He felt ill. "Please?"

She hesitated for a moment and then nodded. "Okay."

"Thanks, sweetheart." He hugged her and pressed a kiss to her temple.

They waited for Stacy to go upstairs to do her homework before making the subversive call. Grady paced restlessly back and forth across the kitchen floor, listening to Hilary's end of the conversation while she talked to Julie's mother.

"Hello, Mrs. Hunter? This is Hilary Campbell.... That's right, I'm Ree." A puzzled look crossed her face and was replaced by one of utter shock. "Ex—excuse me?" she squeaked in a high voice that didn't sound at all like Hilary.

Her mouth dropped open, closed again, and then she gulped. "Pardon me?" Her face turned a remarkable shade of red. It was interesting, since Grady had never seen her blush before. "No, Mrs. Hunter...Mavis... Nothing's been settled yet. No, we haven't... No, I haven't... I really haven't given it any thought.... Yes, she's darling...." The red drained from her face as suddenly as it had risen. Her mouth opened and closed several times as she tried to speak. Finally, she managed to force out, "Fine,

Mrs. Hunter...Mavis... That'll be fine.... Thank you...
Goodbye."

When she hung up the telephone, Hilary took a deep
breath and exhaled, rolling her eyes toward the ceiling.

"Well?" Grady asked.

"Would you like to kill your daughter, or shall I?"

"What?"

The color rushed back into her face as she clenched her
teeth and suddenly screamed, "Stacy! Stacy Thompson,
you get your butt down here this instant!"

Grady stared at Hilary. He didn't know where she found
all that voice in that little body. "Hilary?" he choked out
at last. "Is something wrong?"

"Wrong?" she yelled, every bit as loudly as she had
called for Stacy. She began pacing back and forth across
the kitchen floor, just as Grady had done earlier. "Do you
have any idea what she's done?"

Grady grabbed her by the shoulders, stopping the pacing. "What? Tell me, Hilary."

"Mavis Hunter just asked me where I'm registered!"

"What?"

"Registered!" she repeated.

"Registered for what?"

"Wedding presents." She hissed the words as if they were
an obscenity she had no desire to share with the entire
block.

"Wedding pres—? What?" He looked stunned for an
instant, and then his chest shook with a suppressed
chuckle that couldn't be held back, quickly turning into
riotous laughter.

"Mavis Hunter is taking Stacy for Saturday night so that
we can have some time alone!"

Grady laughed harder and Hilary fumed. He threw his arms around her and roared into her shoulder, tears streaming down his face.

"She told Mavis that I'm going to be her stepmother!" She glanced toward the stairs. "Where the hell is she?"

"If she has any sense at all, she's hiding until you cool off!"

"I will never cool off! Stop laughing, Grady! It's not funny!"

"Come on, sweetheart. Let's go finish our coffee." He turned her toward the family room.

"I don't want coffee!" she ground out through clenched teeth. "I want that girl's head on a platter!"

Grady propelled her toward the sofa. He knew he could properly deflect her anger, given long enough. He only hoped Stacy knew enough to stay out of sight until he had.

IT WASN'T UNTIL AFTER Grady and Stacy had gone to bed and Hilary was alone in the family room, working her way through the last of the blue exam books, that she realized she had blindly cooperated in removing Stacy from the house for all of Saturday night. She and Grady alone, with no possibility of intervention, for at least fifteen hours . . . The way things had been going, that was plenty of time for things to get out of control.

In spite of everything she'd told herself about the futility of getting involved with Grady, she had to admit that Paul was absolutely right about the effect Grady had on her. She *was* hot for him. Every time they got into one of those make-out sessions—what a term!—how adolescent!—on this very sofa, her convictions vanished like the Cheshire cat's smile. She wanted more, and she knew Grady certainly did. At some point during the time Stacy was gone, she and Grady were undoubtedly going to make love, which was the next inevitable step in their relationship.

*Relationship!* she thought, horrified by the word that was bound to be her undoing. When had *that* happened? She'd done her best to avert it, but there it was, all over again—another disaster just waiting to happen.

Though Grady swore he was different, that she wouldn't drive him crazy, she knew he was wrong. He was normal and sensible, just like the fiancés, and, just like his predecessors, he was going to reach the point where enough was enough and he would call it quits.

She'd told him so, but he hadn't believed her. What she hadn't said, however, was that she wasn't nearly as concerned about hurting him as she was about getting hurt herself. Grady was different from the others in one critical way. When he broke up with her, she was already sure it was going to hurt more than all the others put together.

She sighed and shook her head sadly. She couldn't stop herself from getting involved with Grady. For that matter, she couldn't even stop herself from making love with him, though she knew it was a bad idea. All she could do was try to prepare herself for—and protect herself against—the inevitable end, when it came.

And it would.

MEANWHILE, GRADY LAY upstairs in bed and considered the weekend ahead. At the same time that he anticipated it eagerly, he was scared. The accusation of being "sex-starved" was just a little too close to the way things really were to suit his peace of mind.

It wasn't that he was sexually inexperienced. He'd been married for twelve years, and there had been other women before Anne—but it had been a very long time.

At first, after Anne's sudden, unexpected death from a cerebral hemorrhage—she'd only been thirty-two at the time—he'd been numb in every imaginable way—emotionally and physically. During that period, he hadn't even noticed other women, let alone wanted one in bed. When he'd finally begun to experience something he suspected was just physical need, he'd felt unfaithful to Anne every time he considered ending his celibacy. By the time he'd come to terms with that, it had become a habit to channel all his energies into raising Stacy, running the house alone, and fulfilling the duties that had come with his promotion into the detective ranks.

The upshot of it was that he hadn't been with another woman since Anne's death. Only Charlie knew the truth, and that was because he'd guessed it. This had prompted Charlie's ill-fated attempt at matchmaking with that friend of Jenny's and the "gift" that had been the cause of his ultimate humiliation the day he'd met Hilary.

If he'd been asked to describe the woman who would finally awaken his libido and make him want to get on with his life, Grady never would have described Hilary. How could he? He'd never met anyone like her before. She fascinated him, and only part of it was that he found himself waiting to see what was going to happen next. He had to admit, though, to himself if not to her, that it was sort of like waiting for a natural disaster to happen.

Thinking about disasters brought him back to where his thoughts had started: Saturday night alone with Hilary. Every time he touched her, he completely lost control—and that was with his clothes on. What could happen when the two of them were naked and in bed was terrifying, given the amount of time that had elapsed since his last act of intimacy. Right now, he was so ready, he didn't know how he was going to make it to the weekend. By

Saturday, he would be like an animal. But, even worse, if he kept worrying about it, he wouldn't be able to perform at all.

Now *there* was a daunting prospect.

THE FOLLOWING DAY Stacy made dinner, prompting Grady to rescind his threat to sell her to the gypsies. He wasn't sure he could have faced two of Hilary's dinners in a row. Maybe he could teach her to cook.

He looked around the kitchen and thought about how much it had cost when he and Anne had remodeled it about a year before she died—the hand-molded Mexican tiles on the floor, the top-of-the-line counters, the eight-dollars-apiece handles on the real walnut cabinets . . .

Maybe he wouldn't teach Hilary to cook.

After dinner, the telephone started ringing with calls for both Stacy and Hilary, reminding him again how young Hilary was. It was like having two teenagers in the house. The thought made him extremely uneasy for a few moments, until Hilary's conversation disabused him of that notion and reinforced her maturity.

"It's your life, Paul, but I don't think it's a good idea giving Marshall another chance. How long has it been?"

She paused a moment, listening, with no sign that she bought a word of what he was saying. "Remember what happened last time? You don't want to go through that again, do you?"

The protest on the other end almost carried to Grady, but he couldn't understand the individual words. He thought he was probably better off that way.

"He's changed." She sounded as skeptical as if she'd just been told that Pittsburgh's three rivers had reversed their course. "In a pig's eye."

Paul's answer was long, and Hilary shook her head and muttered to herself as he spoke.

"Yeah, I'm a fine one to talk about making the same mistakes over and over. I know that. But why would you break up with—" She stopped mid-sentence, as she suddenly became aware of Grady's attention to her end of the conversation. It was clear that she would now guard her words because of him.

"You're in another relationship now, Paul. He's nice to you. Why would you want to throw that away for Marshall?" The way she said Paul's ex-lover's name gave Grady the impression she thought the man was the lowest form of life. "Is this really because the two of you can't go out in public together? *Think* about it, Paul. If that's what it is, you're gonna have to work it out. Getting back together with Marshall is *not* the answer."

She paused for a moment, listening to Paul, obviously dumbfounded by what he was telling her. "He did *what?* Are you sure?" she demanded when she could finally speak. "Is *that* why you're talking about going back to him again?" She listened for a moment before saying, "So what're you gonna do about it? Are you gonna tell . . . ?" Her eyes slid over to Grady, noted his alert attention again, and her voice dropped to a level that could almost be described as furtive. "Look, I'll talk to you about this later, okay? Right. Bye."

After Hilary broke the connection and before Grady could ask her any questions about what Paul had said— not that she could answer them, anyway—Hilary began dialing one of the numbers on the list of messages Paul and Michael had taken for her in her absence. Though Zeke's name was first on the list, she could wait to call him back. All he was going to do was thank her for bailing him out again. She would call Douglas, fiancé number six. But

first, she would call Vincent, whom she hadn't heard from
in ages.

Though there'd been a time when they'd seen each other
on an almost-daily basis—back in South Oakland, when
he'd been sharing an apartment with Zeke—Vincent and
his wife Tanya had pretty much dropped out of circulation since having the baby. Hilary was sure the added re-
sponsibilities and expenses of parenthood had played a
part in curtailing their social life, but she'd also sensed they
didn't *want* to go out and party as much as they had before. They'd settled down, become domesticated.

In spite of all the changes, Vincent and Tanya still tried
to maintain some contact with their friends from their
prebaby days. As they'd quickly discovered, the best way
to do that was to make it to one of the Fringe Element's
performances every six weeks or so. In addition to being
friends with the members of the band, most of their other
old friends would be there, so they could count on seeing
everyone at the same time. Since Hilary wanted to see
them both and knew how seldom they ventured out anymore, it wasn't difficult for Vincent to persuade her to
bring Grady and meet them at the club out in Regent
Square, where the band was playing the following night.

Vincent's timing couldn't have been better, as far as
Hilary was concerned. Taking Grady to Regent Square
would give him the opportunity to see her in her natural
habitat, so to speak, before they did something irrevers-
ible. If anything would impress upon him the differences
between them, the Regent Square crowd would. They'd
certainly had that effect on the fiancés.

As if the fates were cooperating for once, conspiring to
warn Grady to run for the hills before it was too late, the
call to Douglas revealed that he was re-engaged and
wanted her to meet his new fiancée—why, she wasn't pre-

cisely sure. After juggling some other potential dates, she finally suggested he bring the new fiancée to Regent Square, too. She had to admit she was a little surprised when he agreed.

Later that night, Hilary lay awake and told herself over and over that she was just doing what had to be done. The sooner Grady got the point and broke off their relationship, the less painful it would be.

The problem, she knew deep down inside, was that it was already much too late for either of them.

THE FOLLOWING DAY, it was Charlie's turn to testify in the Connors case and Stacy went to school, leaving Grady and Hilary all alone in the house. While Hilary had been preparing herself mentally for this eventuality, she hadn't considered that she might be faced with it before Saturday. Regardless of what she'd expected, it was only Friday and she and Grady were entirely without a chaperon. From the gleam of tentative anticipation in his eyes, she knew he was aware of it, too.

As he started in on his third cup of coffee, looking like the cat who was thinking about eating the canary, Hilary gave him her most ingenuous smile and offered to pack him a lunch to take to work.

While he didn't buy her feigned ignorance for an instant, Grady thought about letting her make his lunch anyway, just to see what he ended up with. It might not be edible, but it was bound to be interesting. "I've been assigned to protection duty for the day. Officially, I'm all yours."

"If there are important things you need to do down at the station," she offered, "I promise I'll stay right here and work on my dissertation. I won't even answer the door."

He shook his head and suppressed a smile. "Not a chance. We don't know any more about this extortion case than when we started, and Forensics couldn't come up with anything on that threat note."

Hilary chewed on her lower lip, wishing she could re-assure him and then send him off to work for the day. If Paul was right about who he believed had been black-mailing Ryan—and it seemed more than likely that he was—the threat against her could be written off as noth-ing more than a hollow bluff, the last-ditch effort of a man who didn't really have the guts for a face-to-face confron-tation. "And if I tell you that I'm sure I'll be absolutely fine . . . ?"

"Unless you're going to tell me something more sub-stantial than that . . ."

She sighed. "You know I can't, Grady."

He sighed, too. "Then you know I'm not leaving you."

Under the circumstances, there was only one thing Hil-ary could do: get them out of the house as soon as possi-ble and keep them away until school let out for the day. Insisting that she needed to pick up her mail and clothing for their night out at Regent Square, Hilary dragged Grady over to the firehouse. Paul was in the middle of baking éclairs, and Hilary insisted that they stay for the pastries' completion.

While the éclairs were in the oven and Grady was in the living room, playing toss-the-sock with Hamlet, the Great Dane, Hilary cornered Paul for a less-guarded continua-tion of their conversation of the evening before.

"Let me tell Grady the truth," she said bluntly.

Paul shook his head adamantly. "He's scared now, which is what we hoped for when Ryan went to the cops. He doesn't want to go to jail any more than Ryan wants a trial to send him there."

"But does he want it enough to stop?"

"It sure looks like it."

"For good?" she added.

"It looks enough like it that Ryan's talking about asking the police to drop the investigation."

"I don't know if they're gonna drop it that easily, Paul. And it isn't just because they've got so much invested in it at this point, what with guarding me and all."

"You think Grady's sending them a bill?" he asked with a wry smile.

"That's beside the point, and you know it. Everyone clear up to the commissioner's got a stake in it now. They might not be willing to forget it, even if Ryan is."

"Damn him, anyway."

"Damn him is right."

GRADY HAD TO ADMIT the éclairs were worth waiting for, though the entire morning was lost in the waiting. He also had to concede that, with a chef like Paul as a roommate, it was no wonder Hilary had never learned to cook. Why try and compete with perfection?

After they left the firehouse, with a tin of éclairs for later, Hilary estimated that she still had three more hours to fill before Stacy's return from school. With a well-concealed grin of satisfaction at her ingenuity, she hauled Grady across town to Bloomfield. It took more than a half hour to find a parking space, as she'd known it would, and the next two hours were spent poking through the thrift shops and used-book stores that dominated the neighborhood.

Although Grady was frustrated by her transparent efforts to keep them with other people, he had a good time. In all the years he'd lived in Pittsburgh, he'd never been in any of these stores. In fact, he'd never known they existed. He regretted that oversight now, because it was fun poking through the junk in search of "treasures." Apparently Hilary did this often, because the proprietors welcomed her eagerly, lavishing attention on her as if she were a favorite daughter. They made certain she saw the cashmere sweater with the bugle beads, the Victorian amethyst-and-marcasite necklace, and the Art Deco lamp they had just acquired; and they plied her with cake and cookies, and coffee and iced tea.

In these familiar surroundings, Hilary seemed to forget her apprehensions completely. She accepted the fingers that he casually laced through hers while they walked, his light caresses on her arm and back, and the playful kisses that he planted on her nose, her temple, and her hair.

Grady was gratified by her easy acceptance of his affectionate touches, and when she relaxed and started to return the simple gestures, he was delighted. He had already known, from her responses during the past several days, that she wanted him as much as he did her. Now he knew she was also starting to care. He was making progress—real progress.

By the time they returned to the house, they had arrived at a comfortable accord. They emptied their "treasures" out of the hatchback and toted them into the house, eager to show a bewildered Stacy their haul. All right, so it wasn't like him to pay real money for a silver-plated Art Nouveau mantel clock that didn't tell time anymore. They didn't even have a mantel to put it on.

EXCLUSIVE PRIZE # YB 551518

# BIG BUCKS

**$**

*TWO WAYS TO WIN BIG BUCKS!*

**1.** Uncover 5 $ signs in a row . . . BINGO! You're eligible to win the $1,000,000.00 SWEEPSTAKES!

**2.** Uncover 5 $ signs in a row AND uncover $ signs in all 4 corners . . . BINGO! You're also eligible for the $100,000.00 EXTRA BONUS PRIZE!

*HURRY!*
*This Jack Pot must be claimed!*

Scann Here →

LUCKY CHARM GAME!

Claim up to 4 FREE books AND a FREE Mystery Gift!

**YES!** I have played my Big Bucks game card as instructed. Enter my Big Bucks Prize number in the MILLION DOLLAR Sweepstakes and also enter me for the Extra Bonus Prize. When winners are selected, tell me if I've won. If the Lucky Charm is scratched off, I will also receive everything revealed, as explained on the back of this page.

142 CIH AH3R
(U-H-T-03/93)

NAME _____

ADDRESS _____ APT. ____

CITY _____ STATE ____ ZIP ____

**NO PURCHASE OR OBLIGATION NECESSARY TO ENTER SWEEPSTAKES.**

© 1993 HARLEQUIN ENTERPRISES LTD.

**WHY WE GIVE FREE BOOKS AND GIFTS** There's no catch! We give away FREE BOOK(S) and a FREE GIFT to interest you in the Harlequin Reader Service®, but you are under no obligation to buy anything...EVER! You may keep your FREE BOOK(S) and gift and return the accompanying statement marked "cancel." If you do not cancel, approximately a month after you receive your free book(s), we'll send you 4 of the newest Harlequin Temptation® novels and bill you just $2.44 each plus 25¢ delivery and applicable sales tax, if any.* You may cancel at any time by dropping us a line or returning any shipment at our expense!

* Terms and prices subject to change without notice. Sales tax applicable in NY.

# BUSINESS REPLY MAIL
FIRST CLASS MAIL   PERMIT NO. 717   BUFFALO, NY

POSTAGE WILL BE PAID BY ADDRESSEE

"BIG BUCKS"
MILLION DOLLAR SWEEPSTAKES
3010 WALDEN AVE.
P.O. BOX 1867
BUFFALO, N.Y. 14240-9952

NO POSTAGE
NECESSARY
IF MAILED
IN THE
UNITED STATES

# 6

THE INSTANT THAT GRADY and Hilary entered the club that evening, the sense of contentment he'd been cultivating all day was shot right to hell. He didn't need to be told he didn't belong in any bar that catered to people with multiply pierced ears, particularly when those people were male. Although Hilary wore a conservative sundress, she still fit in, simply because she didn't appear to notice how strangely others were dressed. The raucous cry of welcome from a mobbed table in one corner acted as another reminder that this was her crowd. As he and Hilary headed in that direction, Grady noted with some relief that most of the people in that particular group were relatively normal-looking. No spiky green hair, he thought as he eyed one young man at a nearby table who fit that description. No safety pins in noses. No signs that anyone there was strung out on some illegal substance his sense of duty wouldn't allow him to ignore. Thank God.

He was still grappling with the sensation of being out of his element—and the accompanying urge to return to his own quiet house—as room was made for them. A harried-looking waitress took his order for a beer, accepted Hilary's nod as a meaningful request, and set off through the crowd toward the bar. Since the only person Grady knew at the table was Zeke Murdough—now *there* was a comforting thought—she began introductions, but only got halfway around before being sidetracked. It was just as well, as far as Grady was concerned; there were far too many names for him to remember, let alone match them with the corresponding faces.

"I'm so glad Ree brought her own keeper tonight," the dark-haired woman next to him confided as Hilary got caught up in a heated debate over whether someone named Ice something was a true musician or a scam artist. "Frankly, one of them is all I can—or really want to—handle at a time."

She seemed to think Grady should understand what she was talking about. When it was clear that he didn't, she laughed and said, "You don't know, do you?"

In a daze, Grady shook his head. "I'm sorry, I don't."

"That's all right—I understand," she consoled him. "I'm Tanya, Vincent's wife. We don't go out much anymore. Not since we had the baby. But Vincent and Ree are such a treat to see together, we still try and make it every month or so."

The drinks came then. The waitress put a shot glass, a wedge of lemon, and a glass of draft beer in front of Hilary. Tanya caught the look Grady gave them, and correctly interpreted it as a cross between horror and confusion. "Vincent and Ree always drink shots together. It's more for Vincent, really, gutless wonder that he is. He'll chicken out if he doesn't have a few good drinks under his belt first."

*Chicken out from what?* Grady wondered, but he didn't ask. Once again, he wasn't sure he wanted to know.

"It keeps Vincent company," she added. "Generally I have to haul both of them home, and then deal with their hangovers the next morning. It's worth the aggravation, but I can't say I'm sorry someone else is gonna get Ree out of here tonight. Vincent's a handful all by himself."

Even more perplexed than before, Grady silently sipped at his beer and started wondering about Hilary's assertion that he was too sensible and staid to become—and stay—involved with her. Maybe what she'd really meant was that she believed she'd get bored with his ordinariness sooner or later. Was she trying to tell him she actually wanted a man like Zeke Murdough or Vincent or one of the others at the table?

Looking at Grady's uneasy visage and interpreting his discomfort as distaste, Hilary assured herself that bringing him to the bar and exposing him to this group of friends had been the right thing to do. If he was going to have second thoughts about the relationship and jump ship, she'd rather have him do it now, before they'd made love. And, judging by the expression on his face, he just might.

That these were the most outrageous friends she had was to be expected, considering that the core of this crowd was the band performing that night. The Fringe Element was one of the hottest new groups in Pittsburgh, and they were in demand for almost two hundred miles around. There was even some talk of a recording contract, if anyone in the band could summon the discipline to write enough original songs for a whole album.

But maybe she'd owed it to Grady to give him some prior warning, Hilary thought as she reached over to pat him on the knee. "We're all friends of the band," she explained. "They lived in our building when we all lived in South Oakland."

"Oh."

"Vincent lived with Zeke, some of the guys in the band lived upstairs, Scott and . . ." Going around the table, she accounted for everyone's whereabouts four years earlier. "It was an awful building, but we used to have some really great parties—we'd put the stereo speakers in the windows and barbecue out in the parking lot."

"Great fun," agreed Vincent, from the other side of Hilary. He looked vaguely familiar to Grady, but he couldn't think where he might have met Vincent before that night. Things being what they were with Hilary—and considering that he'd lived with Zeke Murdough—Grady tried to visualize him in a lineup. It didn't help.

"You started without me," Hilary accused Vincent. It was obvious from the flush on his face that he'd had a few drinks before their arrival.

"I'm bigger than you are."

"And I have a better tolerance than you do. If you don't slow down, you're not gonna make it to the eleven o'clock show."

"I'll make it." Vincent jutted out his chin impudently. "I promised I would."

"Better slow down, then. You're getting old—can't drink like you used to."

"*I'm* getting old? You're older than I am, and don't you forget it!"

"Only six days."

"You're *still* older."

Tanya watched her husband and Hilary with a tolerant amusement that gradually transmitted itself to Grady. He started to feel a little less self-conscious and nervous, particularly since Hilary's hand still rested reassuringly and somewhat possessively on his knee. He reached down and took her hand in his own, lacing their fingers together against his inner thigh. She not only left it there, she gave his hand a gentle squeeze.

The band began their first set at ten o'clock. Even though their music was something Stacy would have liked more than he did, Grady had to admit that they were good—very good. He'd never been "with the band" before. It was interesting. Everyone at the table knew the program as well as the band members did and cheered enthusiastically after each song. They all talked animatedly and simultaneously and, when they went out on the floor to dance, it was hard to say exactly who was with whom.

Dance. Oh, God, he hadn't even considered that. Grady hadn't danced to anything contemporary since just after Stacy was born. He'd been twenty-five then. After that, he and Anne had confined themselves to nice, conservative slow dances at the occasional wedding or dinner dance. He probably should have taken up Stacy's offer to reteach him how to dance. Hilary's hand fidgeted in his, and he knew she was just itching to get out there on the floor with everyone else. He felt horrible. His hands started to sweat. He thought he was going to be sick.

"Grady, is something wrong?" Hilary shouted the words directly into his ear over the sound of the music.

He shook his head quickly, not wanting to admit the truth.

"Are you sure? You don't look very well!"

He hesitated for an instant and then nodded, trying to smile. Hoping it would change the subject, Grady slid his chair closer to hers and slipped his arm around her waist. To his relief, she shifted in her chair to accommodate him. He hoped they'd play something slow eventually, but he didn't count on it.

Hilary patted his knee again in reassurance, leaning her body against his side. Instinctively, she knew what was wrong. It had never even occurred to her, although it probably should have. Grady didn't know how to dance; at least he hadn't danced in so long, he thought he didn't know how to dance anymore. She'd bet good solid money that the last time he danced, it was to the Who . . . the first time around. She hoped she'd be able to get him out on the floor when the guys played something tame. Maybe Starship. After all, they had evolved from Jefferson Airplane, and that was probably familiar territory for him.

Suddenly the Fringe Element began the first notes of Guns 'n' Roses' "Patience." Hilary had completely forgotten that the band had added them to their program, but she remembered now that they had been working on several different numbers. It was perfect.

"Grady... would you—"

"Hilary... would you like to dance?"

They'd both spoken at the same time and laughed lightly as they realized they'd had the same thought.

"Would you like to dance, honey?"

Grady and Hilary danced together for the first time. Her arms were looped around his neck while his encircled her waist. Her forehead barely reached the top of his chest, and his hands easily spanned her back.

When Grady lowered a kiss to the top of her head, Hilary craned her neck to look up at him and smiled before playfully burying her nose in his chest. He bent his knees slightly, trying to lower his face to the level of hers, but the lowest he could get was her temple. "Hilary, you're not cooperating."

"Hmm?" She lifted her face.

"That's the idea, sweetheart." He caught her mouth with his. "Mmm... you taste good, like lemon...."

The kisses they exchanged were light, promising more. More might have followed if it hadn't been for Vincent's untimely interruption. "Hey, Ree, we got to get moving."

Tanya, behind him and tugging on his arm, was protesting vigorously between clenched teeth. "Vincent, please... Let them finish the dance."

Grady straightened his knees.

"Ree...."

"Vincent, if you don't leave them alone..."

"Tanya, it's—" His words were cut off when his wife firmly gripped his shirt collar and dragged him to the far side of the room.

"Have we just received a reprieve?" Grady asked, lowering his head again to whisper in her ear.

"I think so. Once Tanya has him by the throat, he has to behave."

"What's he so excited about, anyway?"

She rose up on her toes to press another soft kiss on his lips. "Just wait. You'll see."

He bent his knees again and pulled her more closely to him, where he had wanted her in the first place. "I can wait." He didn't mean just for the surprise.

She snuggled into him, tightening her arms around his neck.

When the song finished, the band took a break and they headed back to the table, their arms around each other's waist. Grady sank into his chair, pulling Hilary down on his lap so their faces were level again. "That's better."

It wasn't, because Vincent grabbed Hilary by the arm almost immediately, dragging her away as Grady stared after them.

"What's all this about?" he asked Tanya.

"I'm not telling," Tanya answered, smiling and shaking her head slowly. "You'll see soon enough."

"You must be Grady," a deep voice behind him said.

Grady turned in his chair to face the new arrival. This man, and the woman with him, looked as if they belonged here even less than Grady did. "That's right."

"I was talking to Stephen yesterday and he mentioned you. I'm Douglas."

"Victim number...?"

"Six. You've been to bail out one of her friends already. How long have you known Ree?"

"Since last week."

"And you've got that look already? Poor man. This is Karen."

"Your fiancée." At the puzzled look, Grady added, "I was in the kitchen when Hilary was talking to you."

"What are the damages so far?"

"Damages?"

"She hasn't tried to cook, then. Do yourself a favor, don't let her."

"Are you the bread dough in the oven?"

"No, that's Alex. I'm the turkey with the bag still in it."

"Oh, God." Grady cringed at the thought.

"That's exactly what I said when I found it." Douglas looked around the room, studying the faces in the mob. "Nice crowd," he commented sarcastically, eyeing a blonde with a pink streak in her hair and shaking his head.

"Douglas, why are we here?" Karen asked waveringly.

"Just wait a minute, Karen, you'll see." Douglas settled them both into vacant chairs.

The band returned to the stage, but didn't start until the lead singer spoke into the microphone. After introducing himself and the other band members, he grinned impishly. "We have something special tonight!" Several isolated cheers rippled through the crowd. "After an absence of six weeks, Mick and Tina are back with us again!" The cheers were less isolated and the band started the opening for the Rolling Stones' "Beast of Burden." "Mick and Tina!"

Two figures entered the stage from opposite sides, dancing toward each other as they sang. The man wore tight white knit pants, a red athletic shirt, and high-top sneakers, untied. It was Vincent, and Grady knew instantly why he'd looked so familiar before. He could have been Mick Jagger's clone, and in his costume the resemblance was so obvious, Grady wondered why it hadn't occurred to him before.

The woman was Hilary, garbed in what was obviously the pile of black leather Grady had seen in her room the day he and Charlie had gone to the firehouse. Now, it had been transformed into a miniskirt, a scarf tied around her hips sarong-style, and an oversize motorcycle jacket that hung open over a red top just like the one she'd been wearing that first time Grady had seen her. She also wore a pair of red pumps with astronomically high heels. Her hair had been teased and somehow lacquered in place. He could have sworn it also had a reddish tinge to it.

Grady couldn't figure out how she could possibly have gotten into the tight leather skirt. And he couldn't imagine how she could stand in heels that high. He had never seen her in anything except flat shoes.

He thought she looked absolutely fabulous.

"You haven't seen this before, have you?" Douglas's voice reflected his amusement at the stunned expression on Grady's face.

Grady shook his head, not taking his eyes from the stage as he gaped at Hilary. "I didn't even know..."

If Douglas answered him, Grady didn't hear it. He was mesmerized by the performance on stage. Vincent and Hilary were quite remarkable together. They danced and vamped and played off one another as if they'd been doing it for years, which they probably had. Hilary untied the sarong seductively and hung it around Vincent's neck like a scarf. Vincent did the Mick Jagger pout and strip-teased his shirt. It was entirely too soon when they finished three songs and abandoned the stage to the band again. They left the audience screaming as they raced toward the table, still dressed in their costumes.

Hilary's face glistened triumphantly and she stroked her fingers over her cheekbones, wiping away the perspiration. Grady dug into his back pocket and offered her his handkerchief, which she took gratefully and used to mop her face and chest.

"You were wonderful," Grady told her, his eyes riveted to the thin trickle that ran down the front of her top between her breasts. He wanted to follow it with his fingertips—or his tongue—as well as his eyes.

"Thanks," Hilary replied, her breasts heaving as she struggled to regain her breath.

Grady's own breathing became a struggle as Hilary moved and he got a glimpse inside the leather jacket. Her soft breasts, straining against the damp cotton knit, were clearly outlined. Feeling the sudden tightening at the front of his jeans, he pulled Hilary onto his lap to conceal it. He slipped his arm around her waist, inside the steamy atmosphere of the jacket. Her back was soaked and he pulled the satin lining away from her, allowing air to flow over the bare, moist skin.

Hilary arched her back, and sighed blissfully at the sensation of Grady's hand and the cool air against her fevered skin. A shiver passed through her and her nipples hardened against her top. She picked up Grady's beer from the table and took a long gulp before running the cold glass over her flushed face.

Grady lowered his lips to her face and sipped the condensation as it dripped off her jaw. Hilary closed her eyes and slumped against the solidity of his chest until her mouth was where her jaw had been. She could taste the salt of her own perspiration on his lips and ran her tongue over them as if retrieving what was hers. His tongue met hers and thrust between her parted lips as he pulled her more firmly onto his lap. Her hip was tight against his swollen groin and she turned her body to press her breasts against his chest.

Neither was aware of the crowd around them or the loud music of the band. All they sensed was one another—damp nylon against denim, cool hands on hot back, hard desire against soft hip, and lips and tongues hungrily meeting each other. It was forever before they came back to earth and the reality of the Regent Square bar. Reluctantly they pulled apart, still gazing into each other's eyes with an unspoken promise to continue this later, once they were alone.

Tanya's voice cut through the fog surrounding them as she accused her husband, "You don't kiss me like that anymore."

"Let's buy you a leather outfit like Ree's and then try it. Looks like fun."

Grady and Hilary both raised their heads, looking at the other couple sheepishly. Vincent laughed uproariously. "You two look like you got caught with your hands in the cookie jar."

Grady considered the exact location of his hands and left them inside the back of Hilary's top anyway. He was afraid that if he took them out, she'd stand up.

She reached over for the glass and he quickly moved one hand around to the front of her. Apparently, having his hands inside the back of the top—he still thought it looked like an overgrown bra—had pulled up the front, as well. He tugged the bottom band back into place.

"Thank you," she whispered to him, after taking a sip from the glass.

"Don't these things ever stay where you put them?"

"I never had a bit of trouble with one until last week."
She offered him a sip from the glass and he took it, think-

ing he needed a cold shower more than he needed a cold drink.

"What are you two whispering about, over there?"

"Vincent, you don't have a romantic bone in your whole body," Tanya complained.

"That's not what you said last night."

"That's not romance, you fool. That's lust."

"You weren't complaining then." Vincent glared at Grady in reproach. "Do you realize the trouble you're causing me?"

Grady wasn't sure what Vincent's problem was, but he knew exactly the trouble Hilary was causing him. If she shifted on his lap once more, they were going to have to wait until the place closed before they could go home. As if she had heard his thoughts, she pressed her hip against him again. He groaned, leaning his head on her shoulder. "Stop that!" he hissed.

"Think about your garbage disposal," she suggested.

"I won't have to if you just stop fidgeting!"

"Be nice to me or I'll stand up," Hilary threatened.

"You wouldn't dare!" As if he was afraid she might, his hand closed over the back waistband of her skirt. It kept her there, but it wasn't a great idea. He turned his head and started to talk to Vincent, hoping the distraction would be sufficient to allow them to get out of the bar before Christmas.

Hilary grinned at the animated conversation between Grady and Vincent. They really seemed to like one another, she realized with more than a little astonishment. None of the fiancés had ever taken to Vincent like this. They'd always seemed to be threatened by the way she and Vincent acted onstage, and they hadn't understood that the erotic play between them was limited to their act. If she was any judge of Grady's reaction to it—and her current position more than qualified her to judge—the whole thing had really turned him on.

She studied Grady covertly, wondering at the way he had acted ever since she'd arrived at his house. He'd put up with it a lot—because it meant he could be with her. She knew he understood her—in spite of the flakiness, the total lack of discipline, and the absolute insanity.

And suddenly, the certainty that she was going to make Grady crazy and he was going to throw her out didn't seem nearly as important as the anticipation of making love with Grady. In fact, she found herself wondering why she had believed it was necessary to run him all over the city all day when they'd had an empty house. If she hadn't been such an idiot, they would have been lovers already.

Maybe, just maybe, she thought hopefully, this time they might be able to make it work.

"HILARY?"

"Hmm?" Pulling herself the rest of the way out of the half-asleep state, she opened one eye and peered across at Grady, who was sitting in the driver's seat of the Mazda.

"We're almost home, honey. You look like that tequila did you in."

"To be honest with you, I think it was that steam bath of a jacket."

"Looked great, though." Grady wiggled his eyebrows and leered playfully.

"You *did* seem to like it." She opened the other eye and looked out at her surroundings, which weren't moving. "How can we be almost home? The car's not going anywhere."

"If I know my daughter, we've got a reception committee back at the house." He reached out one hand to touch the stiff fringe of her hair. "Why's your hair so . . ."

"Crisp?" she offered helpfully when he hesitated, apparently struggling for an accurate descriptive word.

"Exactly."

"About a pound of gel. I can hardly wait to wash this sticky mess out."

"Can you wait a few more minutes?"

"Any particular reason?"

"I just want to kiss you once tonight without an audience."

Grady's hand slipped around to cup the back of Hilary's head, pulling her toward him as he leaned across the middle of the car. The first touch of his lips was light and tender, a tantalizing brush across her mouth. The second was pure torture. Drawing her lower lip between his teeth, he tormented it until an eager groan escaped her and Hilary strained to take his mouth more fully. The tingling sensation that had begun at Grady's first touch spread steadily throughout her body, making her hand tremble as it lifted to his jaw.

With a single finger, Hilary traced the path from ear to raging pulse to chin until Grady caught her wrist, dropped a kiss there, and brought her hand around to the back of his neck. As their mouths reunited, her fingers tunneled reflexively through the dark curls, matching the firm hold he had on her nape.

As the kiss deepened, Grady's tongue taunted Hilary's and she responded, the strokes mimicking the intimate act both of them knew was as inevitable and natural as the tide. This substitute wasn't enough for either of them, and their bodies strained toward each other, rubbing against one another, disregarding the two thin layers of cloth that separated Hilary's swollen breasts from the dark, curly mat of hair that covered Grady's chest.

"Oh, Hilary..." Grady murmured, burying his face in the side of her throat, nuzzling her just below her ear. Gratified by her shuddering sob, he eased himself back just enough to burrow his hand underneath the hem of her top, his fingers slipping over the silky skin toward the crest of her breast.

Hilary's head lolled back against the seat as she submitted to the pleasure of Grady's caress, allowing the waves of glorious feeling to flow over her with his touch on her sensitized flesh. All her attention focused on the palms that ran over her breasts, the fingers that kneaded her engorged nipples, and the lips that closed over one, sucking hungrily. She felt as if she'd been struck by a bolt of lightning and she arched her body upward toward him. He captured the nipple in his teeth and teased it with his tongue as the hardness of his lower body ground against the soft leather that covered the center of her femininity.

"Grady... Oh, God...." she moaned, burying her face in his hair as her hand worked itself lower, sliding over his hipbone as she sought the throbbing evidence of his desire. She palmed him through the denim and traced his outline with her fingers.

"Oh, God.... Don't, Hilary!" Grady cried. "Please don't! I... Oh...Hilary!"

The sharp rap on the roof of the car scarcely penetrated through the passion gripping them both. The sudden glare of a flashlight in Hilary's eyes brought her to earth with an astonished gasp. The abrupt stiffening of her body against his alerted Grady that they were no longer alone.

"Okay, kids," a weary voice outside the half-open window demanded. "Break it up. Let's see some ID."

Hilary and Grady both groaned with embarrassment and flushed violently. He tugged down the hem of her top and shifted away slightly. In his current state, he couldn't roll over and retreat to the driver's seat, particularly not under the incriminating circle of light that beamed into the car.

The blue-clad police officer looked down through the window at the tangle of leather and denim and nylon-clad legs. The passenger seat was tilted back to its most horizontal position. He sighed and muttered, "Damn kids. Okay, I asked for some ID."

Grady dug into his back pocket for his wallet, handing it out the window to the officer as Hilary's free hand—the other one was trapped beneath Grady—groped on the floor of the car in search of her purse. Finding it, she pulled it onto her lap and floundered inside for the driver's license she knew was floating around in there somewhere. She was at once annoyed and relieved when the probing light she was using to see into her purse moved away as the officer looked at Grady's license.

He appeared totally confused. What the hell...? "Couldn't wait until you got home, buddy?"

Inside the car, Grady groaned miserably. He was still unable to move back to the driver's seat with anything approaching dignity. Finding her own driver's license, Hilary thrust her hand through the window, but the officer was too preoccupied with Grady's to notice.

He looked at the picture and blinked with surprise. "What the hell?" he asked again before he flipped over the driver's license and looked at the badge inside the wallet. "Detective Thompson?" he asked warily, leaning down to the window of the car as he tried to peer at Grady's face, still buried against Hilary's shoulder.

Grady gulped and swore before turning his head toward the light.

"Detective Thompson?" the voice on the other side of the light repeated, rising uneasily.

Grady nodded reluctantly. Hilary's hand still dangled out the window, her license in it.

"Oh, for..." The light moved away from the window and Grady's wallet was slapped into Hilary's palm. "Sir, I'm sorry," the embarrassed voice continued. "Please...just tell me she's of age and then take her home."

Hilary was grateful it was only a short ride to Grady's house, because the silence strained between them like a rubber band waiting to snap. *Poor Grady,* she thought to herself. She'd bet her last penny that nothing like this ever happened to him before—even when he was a teenager. He looked so humiliated—even more than he had at the supermarket. Maybe hoping things might work out between them was nothing more than a pipe dream, after all. If only he weren't such a great kisser...

Grady drove in silence, his mind churning furiously as he searched its nooks and crannies for a plan. He wouldn't be able to wait until the following night, knowing Hilary was in the same house. He couldn't remember being so cranked up over a woman, even when he was a teenager. If that blue suit hadn't come along and rousted them, he knew they would have made love right in the front seat of the Mazda. Maybe he should bypass the house and head straight for a motel. Maybe he could sneak her into his room, and Stacy would never know. And even if she did find out, how bad could it be? She was almost a grown-up. He suspected she thought he and Hilary had already made love. She had all but sent wedding invitations to the neighbors, so she obviously liked Hilary. And it wasn't as if he brought women to the house every day. Damn! What did other people do with their kids when they wanted to make love?

Almost before the car came to a stop, Hilary leaped out and sped toward the atrium door. As quickly as he could,

Grady pursued her. Just as he reached the open door, however, he heard Hilary's outraged howl from the family room. "Get out of here! Right now! This minute!"

The low voice that answered her didn't sound at all familiar to Grady. "I'm sorry, ma'am.... I'm going right now."

"Ree! No, Ree! We weren't doing anything...really!" It was Stacy.

"Out! Now! I think you've overstayed your welcome!" Hilary sounded exactly the way she had when she had gone to bail out Zeke and take Manny's fine—full of finely tempered fury and gritty determination.

Grady rushed to the open door, where Hilary, pulled to her full five feet, stood barefoot and straddle-legged glaring at a gawky teenage boy who probably would have been taller than Grady, if he stood up straight. The kid looked scared witless. Scared of a tiny bundle of rage minimally clad in leather. She hadn't hit him—yet.

"But, ma'am..." The kid gulped. Seeing Grady in the door, his eyes grew even wider and he choked out, "Mr. Thompson?"

"Daddy!" Stacy screamed, coming to her feet as she appealed to her father. "We weren't doing anything!"

"Stacy, it's two o'clock in the morning!" Grady yelled, as he suddenly recovered his power of speech. "What's he doing here at this hour?"

"I...I..."

"Stacy, sit!" Hilary commanded. Her eyes glittering angrily, she grabbed the kid by the collar of his shirt and dragged him toward the front door of the house.

"But, ma'am..."

"Ma'am, nothing!" Hilary shouted. "If you call me that again I'm going to deck you! Got it? Out!"

Grady heard the front door open and slam shut. He assumed that Tall, Dark and Gawky was on the outside.

"But, Daddy!" Stacy wailed. "We were only watching television!"

Even Grady was alert enough to notice it wasn't on.

"Stacy, you can't have boys in here when no one else is home! You're only fifteen, for God's sake!"

"Ree had no right—"

"She did the right thing, young lady!"

Hilary stood just inside the door to the front hallway and watched father and daughter shout at each other. Her part in this fiasco was done. Or she *thought* it was, anyway.

Suddenly Stacy turned her attack on Hilary. "You had no right! You're not my mother!"

"She will be, Stacy, and don't you forget it!"

Every drop of color fled from Hilary's face at Grady's words. She forgot to breathe. She wasn't sure, but she thought her heart forgot to beat.

The blood from Hilary's face must have flowed to Stacy's, because she was positively scarlet. One hand flew over her mouth, and a squeak escaped her before she ran from the room. A pounding of footsteps followed as she raced up the stairs.

Grady sank onto the couch. "Damn."

Hilary still stood in the doorway, staring at him. She'd regained her ability to breathe, but she suspected any voluntary action was beyond her. "Grady..." She choked. Obviously, her throat didn't work.

The brown eyes that rose to meet hers didn't help. "Hilary, I'm sorry...."

"I shouldn't have..."

"You did the right thing. Thank you."

"I..."

"Come here, Hilary."

Her legs felt wobbly as she crossed the room and dropped down next to Grady. His arm circled her shoulders companionably, but she buried her face in her hands. "I . . ."

"I really didn't mean to propose to you that way, sweetheart."

"Propose?" Her voice rose a full three octaves and her head snapped up. Obviously, the crowd out at Regent Square hadn't done a thing to discourage him.

"I want to marry you, Hilary."

"You can't mean that, Grady."

"But I do—"

"You can't want to *marry* a woman who destroyed your kitchen—"

"I told you, I don't care about the kitchen."

"A woman with a track record like mine."

"Hilary, listen to me." Abruptly he turned her face toward his. "I want to marry you."

"But—"

"And I'm not going to deal with one of those ridiculous long engagements you've tried before, Hilary."

"But—"

"I love you, sweetheart."

"But—"

"Do you love me?"

She nodded without hesitation, surprising herself. "But—"

"Do you want to marry me?"

After a moment's hesitation, she nodded again. "Yes, but—"

"I'm not going to listen to any more of that crap about you driving me crazy, and I'm not letting you get away from me. If I haven't gone stark raving mad and killed you by now, it isn't going to happen. God knows, you've provoked me enough." He leaned forward and kissed her soundly on the lips.

Hilary blinked at him senselessly. Finally, she found her voice. "Grady, you can't be serious!"

His eyes met hers tenderly. "I have never been more serious about anything in my life."

She gulped. "Does this mean we're engaged?"

Grady shook his head. "I don't *ever* want to be your fiancé, honey. I want to be your husband."

She thought about it for a moment. Oddly enough, it made sense. "Oh."

"Do you want to be my wife?"

"I'll make a lousy wife, Grady. It's all I can do to take care of myself."

"I'll take care of you," he assured her calmly.

"I don't know if I can be a good stepmother to Stacy."

"Honey, she's fifteen. She's bigger than you are. It's not as if she needs someone to tie her shoes and hold her hand while she crosses the street. At this point in her life, you're better with her than I am. I couldn't have thrown out that kid with more style than you did. I think he was more scared of you than he was of me." Grady paused a moment, absently stroking a hand over Hilary's nylon-covered thigh. "Speaking of which, could you talk to her tomorrow?"

"Me? You want me to have a little woman-to-woman chat with her?"

"I don't think I could do it." A pained expression crossed his face. "Would you? Please?"

She was going to regret agreeing to this, she just knew it. It seemed too much like agreeing to her new status as potential stepmother. She hadn't even agreed to marry

Grady, though he seemed to think she had. She sighed. "Okay."

"Thanks, honey." He pressed a quick kiss to her temple. It was affectionate rather than passionate. "I know you can do it."

She wished *she* were so certain—not just about talking to Stacy, but about her own capacity for becoming a wife and, maybe, a mother. In her experience, wives and mothers were women like her own mother and grandmothers—women who could do all those "wifely" and "motherly" things without having to call 911. She tried to picture herself baking Christmas cookies, and it wasn't pretty. Visions of mutant reindeer came to mind.

# 7

WHEN HILARY AWOKE the following morning, she and Grady were fitted together like two spoons in a drawer, her back and bottom tucked snugly against his chest and groin. The weight of his left leg, slung over hers with a casual intimacy that suggested they'd been sleeping like that for decades, pinned her there. His left arm was tucked between her own arm and ribs, enabling him to cup one breast possessively in his palm.

She liked it—a great deal more than she knew she should. She could get used to it, actually, in less time than it would take to repair a wrecked Thunderbird.

The ramifications of that thought were, at best, sobering. No matter what Grady said about wanting to marry her—and as soon as possible, by the sounds of it—she couldn't let herself count on his assurance that he knew what he was doing. Others had been sure before . . . and each of them, sooner or later, had been proven dead wrong. She just wasn't wife-and-mother material, no matter how hard she tried.

As her anxiety grew, Hilary tried to ease out of his embrace without waking him. He didn't awaken, but he didn't let go, either; he just mumbled something unintelligible, tightened his grip, and nuzzled his face into her nape. Abandoning her effort, which had been half-hearted at best, Hilary smiled and snuggled closer, recalling everything Grady had said the night before. The memories sent a wave of tenderness flowing through her.

A distinct feeling of being watched intruded on her pleasant thoughts, however, and Hilary opened her eyes to see Stacy's face, mere inches away, as she crouched next to the sofa, peering at her.

"I thought you were awake, but I was just checking," the girl whispered.

"What time is it?" Hilary whispered back conspiratorially.

"Just before ten. Ree, I'm sorry. I shouldn't have said those things to you last night."

"That's okay, Stace." She felt awkward and a bit silly, carrying on a whispered conversation with Grady's daughter while she was lying in his arms and he was sleeping. *Stacy's eyes look just like his,* she thought idly.

"When Daddy wakes up, tell him I've taken the bus downtown. I should be back by noon, latest."

Hilary nodded.

Stacy reached over to the coffee table and picked up Grady's wallet. Hilary held her breath, praying Grady hadn't left the foil packet in there. For once, to her relief, Providence was with them. All Stacy found was his Kaufmann's credit card, which she flashed briefly in Hilary's face before tucking it away in her pocket. "Tell him I took this, too." Smiling, she added, "See you later, Ree," before coming to her feet.

"Bye, Stacy."

Well, she'd made peace with Stacy, Hilary thought groggily as she dozed off again. It was going to make the little talk she'd promised Grady she'd have with his daughter that much less difficult.

When she woke again, sometime later, it was to the smell of coffee wafting under her nose. Grady's heat was gone from behind her. Opening her eyes, she saw his face looking into hers, exactly where Stacy's had been earlier.

"We're alone," he told her, his eyes glimmering so eagerly, she almost hated to disillusion him.

She sat up, shaking her hair back over her shoulders as she yawned. "Not for long. Stacy's only gone downtown and she'll be back by noon."

"How do you know that?" he asked wonderingly.

"We had a nice chat before she left. Oh, and by the way, she's got your Kaufmann's card."

Grady placed the two mugs of coffee on the table and moved to sit next to her, slipping one arm around her waist and pulling her into a kiss. The kiss was slow, languorous, openmouthed, promising a sequel later, when they knew Stacy wouldn't walk in on them.

Grady didn't want to wait. He wanted her now, sleep tousled and flushed and beautiful. Nuzzling her bare shoulder with his mouth and smiling as he felt the shiver the caress initiated, Grady suggested, "Stacy's seen us sleeping down here so often, I don't think she'd be shocked by our going to bed together. It's ridiculous, isn't it? A four-bedroom house, and we're sleeping on the sofa. It'll change tonight, won't it, sweetheart?"

"Permanently?" she squeaked. He loved the way her voice rose unpredictably when she was nervous. And he knew any suggestion of permanency made her *very* nervous, because she still didn't believe him. It was so frustrating.

"Hilary, I want to hold you while I sleep every night."

"I know, but Stacy—"

"She already thinks we're lovers, darling."

Hilary's head snapped around and her eyes met Grady's. He smiled encouragingly and she returned it with only the slightest hesitation.

"She's not a child anymore. That little scene last night convinced me of that. I know she's old enough to handle it." His eyes were soft, pleading for her agreement.

"We'll see."

The atrium door squeaked as it opened, interrupting them. "Hey, Grady, where are you?" Charlie's voice rang through the quiet house.

"In here, Charlie. I'll be out in a minute. Go on and get yourself some coffee." In a lower voice, he told Hilary, "Why don't you go on upstairs and find some real clothes? I don't think I'm up to the challenge of explaining the leather to Charlie this morning."

Hilary nodded and uncurled herself from the sofa and Grady's arms.

"Hurry back," Grady told her. "And Hilary, I love you."

"I love you, too, Grady," she said softly before going through the front hall and up the stairs.

Grady's eyes followed where she'd gone long after he couldn't see her anymore. A voice from the doorway broke into his thoughts. "Hey, Grady. Wake up."

He turned to look at Charlie.

"I heard the strangest rumor," his partner remarked, almost casually, but not quite. "Something about a red Mazda parked a couple of blocks from here. McKain said there were two people in the passenger seat and—"

"It's all over the station already?" Grady winced as he followed Charlie into the kitchen.

"You think he'd keep a good one like that to himself?" Charlie grinned and shook his head. "It's the first thing I heard this morning—they even called me at home to tell me. What in God's name was Ree wearing? I'm assuming it was Ree, anyway."

"It was. A Tina Turner costume."

"Oh. That explains it, then. He said something about black leather and I thought you'd gone kinky on—"

"Stow it, Charlie."

Charlie did.

BY THE TIME STACY returned from town carrying an ominously full shopping bag, Hilary had donned a pair of full plaid dance shorts and a matching blouse. Bracing herself for the ordeal to come, she tapped softly on Stacy's bedroom door.

Her reception wasn't quite what she had expected. Stacy was bubbly and thrilled to see her, practically dragging her into the room and seating them both cross-legged on the bed. "You've got to see what I bought, Ree! It's great, absolutely great!"

She exuded all the boundless enthusiasm of a fifteen-year-old, and suddenly Hilary felt considerably older than twenty-six. Digging into each of the packages inside the shopping bag, Stacy eagerly showed Hilary her purchases. Hilary liked the yellow blouse and asked if it came in blue. Stacy said it did, but offered to lend the yellow to Hilary if she ever wanted to borrow it. Stacy showed her the clip-on earrings and matching necklace, bemoaning the fact that her father wouldn't let her get her ears pierced. Hilary, fidgeting with one of the diamond studs in her ears, told her she'd see if she could talk to Grady about it.

They also held a somewhat convoluted version of the talk Hilary had promised Grady they'd have. Stacy assured her she wouldn't do anything stupid, and Hilary prayed her idea of "stupid" and Stacy's overlapped.

At last, Stacy whipped out a flat box wrapped in pastel paper and pink ribbon and presented it to Hilary. "I got this for you," she said proudly. "I wanted to make up for being such a pain."

"Stace, you didn't have to—"

"Besides—" she grinned impishly "—I know why Julie's mom's letting me stay at their house tonight. Open it, Ree."

It was the look in Stacy's eyes that worried Hilary. It should have. When she took the lid off the box, she gasped in astonishment. "Oh, Stacy—"

Hilary recognized it immediately. It had been hanging on the front aisle of Kaufmann's lingerie department for the past month. She'd told herself she'd give it serious consideration when it hit third markdown. It was a Christian Dior teddy, all pearl-gray lace and clingy satin as delicate as the tissue it was nested in. And underneath it—dear God—was the comb coat. The girl was going to be real trouble in a couple of years, Hilary just knew it. Instincts that picked out an outfit like this at fifteen were dangerous.

"You like it?" Stacy asked, beaming like a child at Christmas.

"Oh, it's gorgeous, Stacy. You—"

"It'll look great on you, Ree! You're so tiny! Daddy'll love it!"

The enthusiasm was contagious and Hilary grinned back. She couldn't help herself, even though she knew Grady was going to have heart failure when the bill came. She'd have to discuss returning it with him. Meanwhile, she thanked Stacy effusively and took the box with her when she got up to leave the room.

Just before she reached the door, Stacy's voice stopped her. "Ree, you and Daddy don't have to worry about me, 'kay?"

Hilary's eyes met Stacy's. They *were* just like Grady's. "I know, Stace. He's just concerned about you growing up too fast and doing something foolish before you're ready to handle it."

Stacy looked confused for a moment, as if she didn't know what Hilary was talking about, and suddenly a look of enlightenment crossed her face. "Oh! Ree, you two don't have to worry about that! I was just kissing Brandon. And that's all I intend to do, at least for another couple of years. I'm curious, but I can wait. I guess I'm afraid, too, so that means I'm not ready yet. Relieved to hear that, aren't ya?"

Hilary nodded. She had to admit she was.

"What I was talking about, though, was you and Daddy. You don't have to sleep on the couch 'cause of me. 'Kay?"

"'Kay."


"THAT'S SOME KID you've got, Grady Thompson," Hilary told him several hours later, after they had seen Stacy off on her date with Brandon Pengelly. It had been difficult to say whether the boy was more embarrassed or wary, after the night before. Grady was counting on wary.

"Did you two have a nice talk?"

"It was enlightening."

"For which one of you?"

"Me, I think. She told me we don't have to sleep on the sofa anymore."

"I told you she could handle it."

Hilary sighed. "She can *more* than handle it. She bought me a present."

"Oh?"

"Grady, I have to return it. The kid's got good taste, but—"

"She already warned me. Is it worth it?"

"Every penny."

"Then you have to keep it. Do I get to see it?"

"Now?"

"Maybe later." He kissed her gently, pressing his lips to hers for only an instant. "Definitely later." He nibbled at her bottom lip teasingly as he ran one finger along the elastic leg of her bikini panties under the leg of her shorts, thrilling the nerves from the inside of her thigh to the outside of her hip. "Eventually." Then he melded their mouths completely, cupping her hips with his hands.

A pang of anticipation tore through Hilary as she circled Grady's neck with her arms, pulling him closer to her while she returned his kiss greedily.

The sudden movement caused them both to lose their balance and they tumbled back onto the sofa, the lengths of their bodies pressed together. The kiss they shared was gloriously devouring, rich with the passion that had been building steadily in each of them for days. They clutched at one another desperately, unable to get enough of each other.

Grady's lips moved around to the side of her throat, nibbling just under her ear as his hands stroked every inch of her body, moving rapidly from breast to thigh to buttocks to the exquisitely sensitive juncture of her legs. Hilary's movements were just as frantic, her hands exploring him with an intensity that made both of them cry out.

His breath ragged, Grady raised his head from Hilary's throat. His eyes were pained as he looked down at her hungrily. "I wanted it to be slow and perfect the first time, but I don't think I can wait, sweetheart," he admitted, gasping and gulping with the effort of speaking. "It's been too long. So long . . ."

"I know," she breathed, her eyes reflecting desire mixed with understanding. She raised her mouth to his for a bare instant before she pushed up against him and yanked her blouse over her head, heedless of the fact that it had buttons. By the time she reached for the hook at the back of her bra, Grady, sitting next to her on the sofa, was divesting himself of his shirt. It was very nearly a race to see which of them could tear off their clothes more quickly, but Hilary finished first and knelt down on the floor, naked, to work off Grady's shoes and socks while he undid the button and zipper of his jeans.

Together, they stood and eased his jeans and shorts down over his hips before he caught her against him and lowered her to the sofa again, lying between her open thighs as his erection strained against the moist, ready warmth of her femininity. He entered her swiftly and she arched upward against him, crying out wordlessly as he began deep penetrating thrusts and withdrawals in a frenzied rhythm that she quickly adopted, meeting each of his frantic movements with one of her own, her slim legs wrapped around his muscular thighs.

Together, they were transported to a place where only they existed—a glorious place of swirling sensation and fulfillment. They soared there together as if in an endless sky, rising and falling with a rhythm that matched the movement of their bodies.

For Hilary, the culmination began deep inside in a series of spasms beyond anything she had ever known. Great racking tremors shook her as she struggled for each breath, her pulse pounded in her temples, and she clutched at Grady with her arms, her legs, and the depths of her womb. The contractions of her body pulled Grady over the edge with her, and a feral cry of pleasure escaped him as he shuddered against her.

Clinging together and trembling, Grady and Hilary gasped for air and their eyes met as they shared a sense of awe at the splendor they had shared. Simultaneously, they realized they were both weeping tears of joy and began to kiss away each other's tears. Still joined, Grady rolled them onto their sides as they tenderly kissed and caressed.

"I love you, Hilary," Grady whispered, squeezing her waist tightly. "And I'd replace the whole damned kitchen every week to have this for the rest of my life."

"Oh, Grady, I love you, too." Hilary sighed, touching the pulse at his temple with her lips.

"I'm sorry it was so fast. I wanted—"

"Shh," she assured him, stilling his words with her fingers against his mouth. "Next time."

"How would you feel about cooking lessons?" Grady asked tentatively while he poked through the refrigerator later that evening.

"I tried that once."

"And?"

"I was asked never to come back."

"I'll teach you."

"I guess we could try."

He emerged from the refrigerator and gave her a squeeze.

UNDER GRADY'S CAREFUL supervision, Hilary made sautéed shrimp, wild rice and garlic bread. It was the most complicated meal she had ever attempted, and their plans very nearly went awry when they got sidetracked and almost forgot about the shrimp. Hilary had no way of knowing Grady had bought shrimp because he knew there were very few ways she could ruin them in the few minutes it took to sauté them.

He was right. They were foolproof. And Hilary was as thrilled as a child that she had actually made a whole meal without destroying either it or the kitchen. She even turned out to be reasonably proficient at rinsing the dishes and loading the dishwasher, though Grady didn't trust her enough to let her add the detergent and turn the machine on. She was adorable and he loved her, but there was no point in pushing his luck.

As they curled up together on the sofa with the remainder of the wine, Hilary beamed happily. "Thanks, Grady. You're the only person who ever had the patience to teach me how to cook. Paul threatened to throw me out the window if I ever set foot in his kitchen again."

"All you needed was the right teacher."

"How can I ever thank you?"

"We'll think of something," Grady growled huskily, nuzzling her ear.

"Later, Grady. I'm still too full to think about exercise." She patted her flat stomach contentedly and sighed.

Grady blanched and inhaled sharply at the innocent gesture. At his age, how could he have been so stupid? He could only plead intense distraction. "Oh, damn . . ." he groaned.

"Grady? Are you all right? I haven't poisoned you, have I?"

"Everything happened so fast, I never thought to ask, honey. I'm so sorry— Are you on birth-control pills?"

She nodded. "My doctor put me on them a couple of years ago because my cycle was so irregular."

Grady began to breathe again and smiled as he considered her answer. It seemed pointless to make the obvious comment that everything else about her life was irregular, so why should her cycle be any different? It crossed his mind that he'd heard stories about women getting pregnant while they were on the Pill. He didn't have the slightest doubt that, if it was possible, Hilary would accomplish precisely that, given her propensity for calamity. He shrugged and told himself it didn't matter; by the time they would have to deal with the possible failure of Hilary's birth control, they would already be married, if he had anything to say about it.

"I know we haven't talked about it yet, but do you want children?" he asked.

"I don't know.... Maybe someday. I've never really thought about it." Hilary looked a little green at the idea, which told him a lot more than her words did. "Do you?"

Actually, he'd be thrilled, but he wasn't going to let her psych herself out over it. He could tell she was remembering her earlier argument that she wasn't suited to be a wife and mother, and he didn't think it was a good idea to commit himself either way until she came to terms with the subject. "I'd love any child of ours, Hilary, but I'm already bringing Stacy into this marriage. The next one's your choice."

"I don't even *know* any children—except Stacy, and she's bigger than I am, so I don't think I can count her."

"What about Vincent and Tanya's baby?"

"I've only seen him a couple of times. He's little."

"They usually start out that way."

"I know." Her eyes were as big as saucers and her chin looked a little wobbly.

Grady stroked his thumb under her jaw and it helped to settle the trembling. "Honey, I mean it. I want it to be your decision *when* or *if* we have a baby. I'm not going to pressure you into anything you don't want to do. I love you. I want you with me the rest of my life, whether or not we ever have children together."

Hilary's eyes were misty as she gave Grady a tremulous smile and a quick kiss. She was grateful to him for making it her choice, for encouraging her instead of trying to railroad her—at least most of the time. It was the kind of sensitivity that had transformed her attraction to him into love. "Are you sure you're the same guy who threw me over your shoulder?"

He grinned at her. "You asking for another demonstration?"

"I've got a better idea," she said, returning his smile as she came to her feet. "Give me five minute's head start and then bring the wine and meet me upstairs. 'Kay?"

"Does this mean I get to see whether Stacy spent my money wisely?"

Hilary smiled slyly and disappeared up the stairs.

STACY DID HAVE great taste, Hilary admitted several minutes later as she stood on the rim of the tub to look in the bathroom mirror. The teddy was exquisite, silky and clingy, with extravagant openwork lace at the top of the bodice. It had a fitted waist and high-cut legs that angled up sharply at the outside hips. The matching comb coat, just long enough to cover the teddy, hung open over it, enhancing her figure more than it concealed it. The pearl-gray color was perfect for her, too, making her skin seem even more translucent than it was. One of her friends had once said that Christian Dior lingerie made a woman feel like a princess. She was right.

Grady could wait no more than thirty seconds before he went upstairs to his bedroom. He turned down the comforter, exposing the crisp sheets he'd put on the bed that morning in anticipation of the night to come. He started to take off his clothes, thought better of it, and went and brushed his teeth instead. Raking one hand through hair he had combed just before he'd brushed his teeth, he paced from one end of the bedroom to the other, muttering to himself.

He recognized that he was acting like a nervous wreck. Hell, he *was* a nervous wreck. His heart was pounding as if it intended to leave his chest, his mouth was dry, and the rest of him was sweating so much, he felt clammy. For one brief, paralyzing instant, he panicked—if he couldn't remember his own name, how was he going to remember what to do?

Grady caught his breath when Hilary appeared in the doorway. She was absolutely stunning. The whispery excuse for lingerie could have been custom-made for her. It clung lovingly to her soft curves and hollows like a caress. The delicate color made her skin look even more opaline than he remembered, and as fragile as porcelain. He was so awestruck, desire overcame his nervousness. Swallowing with difficulty, he extended one hand toward her invitingly and murmured, "I missed you, sweetheart."

Hilary moved to where he stood, her arms sliding up to loop about his neck. "I missed you, too," she whispered back.

His arms encircled her waist, holding her firmly, but with none of the clutching desperation that had gripped them both earlier. They had all night to make love to each other. This time would be perfect. Slow and perfect.

Hilary raised her face to Grady's and his mouth covered hers in a tender kiss that made her knees forget that their function was to support her. Clinging to his shoulders, she melted against him as his hands roved slowly down from her waist. He cupped the roundness of her buttocks and ran his fingers along the sensitive groove where they met her legs and the teddy ended.

With a slow, shuddering breath, Hilary's mouth left Grady's and caressed his chin, pressing soft kisses there before she began working her way along the underside of his jaw toward his ear. His eyes closed as her tongue began to draw leisurely circles around the rim of his ear, fully aware that it was slow torture for him.

The touch of Grady's hands on the silky fabric was featherlike over Hilary's skin, leaving it clamoring for more as the comb coat floated to the floor. His hands were magic, she decided. They were so strong, and yet so gentle. She whimpered softly against Grady's ear and the sweet vibration tore through him like lightning.

Bending, Grady caught her behind her shoulders and under her knees, swept her up against his chest, and took the few short steps to the bed. Then, lying next to her, he continued to work his magic on her body, finding erogenous zones Hilary had never known had so much potential. With a light touch of his fingers, he explored every inch of her face, tracing from her hairline, over the curve of her nose, and across her parted lips.

Drawing one of his fingers into her mouth, she taunted him, kissing, licking, nibbling, and sucking it in a suggestive manner that enraptured Grady at the same time that it excited him.

"Sweetheart, you're a treasure," he told her softly as he lowered his head and kissed the side of her throat. "So natural, so unspoiled . . . But if you don't stop, I'm going to explode."

Hilary laughed in that low trill Grady loved, lifted her hand to his wrist and gave the finger one last kiss before she moved his hand to lay it flat against the side of her neck. She slowly started to unbutton the front of his shirt, stopping after each button to kiss the newly exposed skin. After the third button, she smiled up at him mischievously and asked, "Better?"

"Seductress," he gently accused as his mouth trailed from her ear to just under the top edge of the teddy, where he nuzzled the soft swells above the lace. His fingers grazed lightly over the creamy skin of her collarbone and down to the tips of her breasts. A shiver swept over Hilary as his thumbs circled the hard buds through the shimmery fabric. "So silky. So . . ."

Grady's next words were forgotten as his lips closed over her nipple. He tugged on it and the sheer satin caught between his lips, rubbing her in a sensual caress. Lifting his head, he blew gently on the damp cloth. A spasm of pleasure tore through Hilary and a low cry escaped her as her flesh tingled in response to the light touch of his breath. She gasped when the warmth of his mouth returned to enfold the taut peak, now bared as he slipped the straps of the teddy off her shoulders.

While Grady's mouth lavished attention on first one and then the other of her breasts, his hand began the slow journey down across her abdomen toward the nest of her femininity. When he found his goal, he cupped it tenderly through the silky fabric, his fingers next to the throbbing pulse that was now the center of Hilary's being. Raising his head from the tip of her breast, Grady pressed yet another kiss to her lips. Then, easing away from her, he slipped the last barrier of clothing down and off her body and sat up next to her, gazing at her lovingly.

Hilary was so beautiful—just the way he'd dreamed she would look in his bed. Her skin was smooth and white, its only color the flush of passion. Her hair lay gloriously spread out over his pillow, her eyes were smoky and slumberous with desire, and her lips were full and red from his kisses.

"Oh, Grady, please love me," she whispered.

His head lowered to kiss her again. "I do, darling, I do."

Slowly, his fingertips brushed over her body, exploring every inch of it with agonizing thoroughness. She had to struggle for every breath and when his touch finally insinuated itself between her thighs, she arched her body against his hand reflexively. "Oh, Grady, I want you inside me," she breathed.

"I am, sweetheart."

"No, Grady..." Hilary felt the beginnings of her climax and she reached for him, her fingers finding the hard fullness of his manhood. "I want... Oh!"

Grady was spellbound by the rapturous expression on Hilary's face. He was also overwhelmed by the knowledge that he had caused it. Her head was thrown back ecstatically, her eyes tightly closed and her lips parted as soft mewls of pleasure escaped them. Although he was aching with desire, watching her gave him a sense of fulfillment that allowed him to set his own needs aside for the moment. He wanted to give her the moon before he joined her there.

When the climax subsided, Hilary wanted more. She wanted Grady with her, in her. She wanted to return to the great soaring place they had found downstairs, the place where they could only go together. She tugged the hem of his shirt free of his jeans. "Grady, please... Come with me...."

Grady rose to his feet only long enough to peel off his clothing and then he was back on the bed with her, covering her body with his. Their bodies melded together, moving slowly at first and then harder and faster as they soared higher. Together, they found the release that carried them to their own special place.

They couldn't get enough of each other. When they weren't actually making love, they were touching and kissing and talking, reluctant to let go of their new intimacy long enough to sleep. Finally, they dozed in each other's arms, waking later to start all over again... and again. Each time, it was different and wonderful, showing them all the aspects of love.

"GRADY, WAKE UP," Hilary said.

"Again?" Grady groaned, burying his head in his pillow. "I'm not going to be able to walk if you don't leave me alone. Do you really want a crippled old man?"

Hilary lifted the edge of the blanket and peered under it consideringly. "Doesn't look crippled to me."

Grady turned his face out of the pillow and clutched the blanket against his chest in a parody of affronted modesty. "Hilary, really! Are you trying to ravish me again?"

"Who was ravishing whom?"

"Maybe it was mutual. Should we try it again and see?"

"I was trying to wake you up," she said innocently.

"I'm awake now."

Hilary chuckled at the lightly suggestive tone of Grady's voice as she bent her head down to press a kiss to his lips. His hands moved to her waist.

"Grady, we'd better not start anything we can't finish—"

"You *do* think I'm a crippled old man!"

"No, darling. Just a man who's completely lost track of time."

"I've had other things to occupy my attention."

"Do you have any idea what time it is?"

He shook his head and grinned happily. "I don't even know what *day* it is."

"I hate to be the one to break the news to you, but it's eleven-thirty on Sunday morning."

"Eleven-thirty?" Grady twisted around to look at the clock as if he didn't believe her. It was eleven-thirty.

"I told you so. I was just waking you up because I thought we ought to be out of bed before Stacy gets home."

"Oh. Good point." Grady knew Stacy was going to want to tell them all about her date as soon as she could. It was one thing for her to say it didn't bother her that Hilary was sharing her father's bed. It was another altogether for her to see them that way in the flesh—and with so much flesh exposed. "C'mon, let's go get a shower."

"Not together."

"We took a shower together last night."

"And, if you'll remember, by the time we finished, we ended up back here and we both needed another shower."

"Oh. Right." Grady grinned at the memory. "Separate showers then, I guess."

"You go first. I'll go make coffee."

"You can make coffee?"

Hilary stuck her tongue out at him. "It's not as good as Paul's, but if you'll recall, I *do* know how to make coffee."

"We'll see." He threw back the covers, swung his legs out of bed, and started toward the bathroom, still naked. A low wolf whistle followed after him, and his head snapped around to its source. "Where did you learn to do that?"

"Paul's latest lover."

Slightly discomfited by the fact that the man who had taught her how to whistle like that was more likely to whistle at *him* than at her, Grady walked the rest of the way to the bathroom and stepped into the shower.

# 8

MONDAY MORNING BROUGHT them all back to the real world. Stacy had school, and Hilary had to go to the university to teach her intro-to-lit class. Hilary had really expected that Grady would accompany her the way he had on Friday, but, announcing in a cheerful voice that he had things to do, places to go, and people to see, he kissed her goodbye and left her with a plainclothes escort.

Since the other policeman had his own car and the Mazda was parked in front of the garage Grady took her car. As he got in, she heard some rude and chauvinistic muttering about women thinking cars were just oversize purses with wheels.

Hilary's day was as much of a bear as she had feared it would be, making her wish she had Grady there for moral support. She always hated returning exams and papers when she knew there was going to be a problem, and she'd known there was going to be a problem this time. She'd been a bit surprised, however, when the telephone in the office she shared with three other graduate students rang a mere half-hour after she'd given Boone Fuller back his exam.

"Hilary Campbell?" a surly-sounding voice on the other end of the line asked.

"Of course it is, Nathaniel." Nathaniel Littman was the academic coordinator for the athletic department, a man with whom Hilary had had a great deal of contact over the past several years. "I've been waiting for you to call. I just didn't expect to hear from you this soon."

"You fail Boone Fuller and you don't think they're going to get upset?"

"I *knew* they were going to get upset. I just thought it would take longer for the boy to remember the words, 'Hey, coach, I failed.'"

"Would it make you feel any better to know he threw the blue book at us and grunted?"

"It wouldn't surprise me in the least. He's living proof of evolution, you know."

Nathaniel's sigh carried through the telephone line. They'd covered this territory before, a number of times, which was why Hilary hoped the permanent teaching position she eventually got was at a school that was less sports-as-big-business oriented. She didn't really want to have to deal with Nathaniel—or his equivalent—for the remainder of her career. "Hilary, are we going to have to go through this again?"

"If you didn't want to go through this again, you shouldn't have given me another one."

"We didn't have a choice. Your class was the only one that fit into his schedule."

"You mean he takes more than one class at a time?"

"Okay, Hilary, let's cut to the chase now. What are you asking for this time?"

"Paris."

"Paris?"

"You gave Linda Moscow." Linda, her friend in the sociology department, taught intro-to-soc classes, but her primary area of research was the changing social structure in what used to be the Soviet Union.

"Oh, for God's sake—"

"Paris," she repeated in a voice that sounded as if it wasn't open to negotiation.

"You're studying *English*."

"I'm studying *literature*. Oscar Wilde worked in Paris, Huysmans worked in Paris—" And Hilary had lived in Paris for a large part of her childhood, when her father had been in charge of the Easterbrook Appliances offices there. She had always wanted to go back again as an adult. If she could manage to do it at someone else's expense, so much the better.

"Okay, okay," he agreed begrudgingly. "Four weeks?"

"Six."

"You've never asked for six before."

"Linda got six. Besides, I have a feeling it's going to take a lot of dragging to get Boone Fuller through this course." Although she knew some faculty members just took the inducement and passed the jocks so they could keep their academic eligibility, Hilary had always been one of those who believed there should be at least some semblance of real tutoring and work involved. Without it, the compensation had always seemed like nothing more than bribery to her. While her ethical standards were flexible, that didn't mean they were nonexistent.

"Okay, okay. Six."

"Tell them I'll start tutoring him next week. This week's all filled up."

"You'll give him an incomplete until you can work his grade up to a C?"

"Against my better judgment, yes."

"I'm glad we didn't have to go over your head again this time."

"I never gained anything by that. I always ended up doing it anyway."

"Hilary, you know how it is."

She sighed heavily, thinking about the grim reality of big-time college athletics and wishing it didn't have to be this way. Maybe she'd be able to get a job at Penn State, where she'd heard Coach Joe Paterno insisted his athletes exercised their minds, as well as their muscles. "Only too well, Nathaniel. I keep telling you to go get a real job, but you never listen to me."

"You don't think it's a real job taking care of this bunch?"

"I'm sure it is," she told him sincerely. A *legitimate* job was another story.

"Thanks. I'll send you the stuff for Paris, then. Talk to you."

"Not if I can help it. Oh, and Nathaniel . . . ?"

"Yes, Hilary?"

"Can you make sure this one has a nice cold shower before you send him over?"

"Hilary—"

"Bye!"

The plainclothes officer who had been sent to guard Hilary was more than a little horrified by the whole discussion. He was even more aghast at the suggestion she spat at the receiver, once it was back in its cradle.

BECAUSE HILARY'S CAR had a slight problem with second gear, it took Grady longer than usual to get to the precinct station. He was late, which was something that was virtually unknown to him. After parking the car in the lot, he ran upstairs and managed, just by the skin of his teeth, to dart down the hall to his office without being seen by Lieutenant Angelucci.

Charlie looked up from his desk, where he was sifting through a veritable mountain of paperwork that had to be collated and filed. "For a while there, I was starting to think we weren't ever going to see you again. Did the K-Car give you trouble?"

"I have Hilary's car. They're promising I'll have the T-Bird back by the end of the week."

"And you believe them? You are so naive, Grady." Charlie grinned mischievously as he picked up a couple of stacks of the unwanted paperwork and dumped them on Grady's desk.

"I think I told you that once, didn't I?" Grady shook his head sheepishly and dropped into the chair, stretching his long legs out in front of him. Yawning and ignoring the reams of paper he'd just been given, he dropped his head back and closed his eyes.

"Tired?"

"Mmm-hmm."

"Happy?"

"Mmm-hmm." He lifted his head and opened his eyes again to smile at his partner. Charlie thought the smile was getting pretty sappy-looking. It looked as if he'd been drinking—heavily—though it was far short of noon. "Might be taking some time off soon."

"You've got enough coming. What is it—seven weeks?"

"Eight." Over the past several years, with no real incentive to take a vacation, he'd let the time accumulate.

"Any special reason?"

"Mmm-hmm."

"Grady, if you don't tell me something pretty soon, I'm gonna beat the crap out of you."

"I was thinking about a honeymoon," Grady said quietly.

Charlie was positively stunned and, for a moment, uncharacteristically speechless. At last, he collected himself and asked, "Have you asked Ree to marry you yet?"

"Mmm-hmm."

"Lord, we're back to that again. She said yes?"

"No."

It didn't sound as if it bothered Grady. He was also starting to talk like the firehouse trio, and that *really* worried Charlie.

"It's kind of stupid to go on a honeymoon without her, isn't it?"

"She also said she wouldn't go out with me, remember?"

"Good point. So when's the wedding?"

"Soon. I'll let you know."

"Grady, this isn't like you."

"I know that." He started to laugh and Charlie began to entertain serious doubts about his partner's sanity.

"Are you sure about this?"

"Yes. I love her, Charlie. I'm not going to let her make me crazy."

"Excuse me?" As far as Charlie could tell, it was already too late.

"I'd rather live crazy than live without her."

"You've only known her a couple of weeks," Charlie pointed out reasonably.

"I know. And it's been the best couple of weeks I can remember in an awful long time."

"What about your kitchen?"

"I'm teaching her how to cook."

"My God, you *are* in love."

"Told you I was."

The telephone rang, interrupting them, and Charlie answered it. It was Jenny. "Hey, honey, wait until you hear this. Grady's getting married."

UNLIKE CHARLIE, Lieutenant Angelucci didn't blink an eye at Grady's surprise announcement that he wanted his vacation as soon as possible. He was far too busy with his fury about solid-as-a-rock Grady Thompson crumbling faster than day-old bread.

"Thompson, you've had a spotless record for fifteen years. What the hell happened?" he asked, more quietly than anyone had ever heard him. That should have told Grady something, but he didn't even notice it.

"I ran the T-Bird into a lamppost."

"I *know* that, Thompson. What I meant was, what's happened since then? I keep getting the most bizarre reports of you turning up in Main Booking to bail out a known criminal, asleep in the courthouse when you're supposed to be there testifying for an important case, at some way-out bar out in Regent Square, and in a parked car in Highland Park, doing God-only-knows-what. On the last two occasions, I might add, your companion was reportedly wearing rather peculiar clothing. What's going on?"

"I'm getting married," Grady replied distractedly.

"We're pleased for you, Thompson. But weren't you supposed to be guarding Jenkins's girlfriend?"

"As soon as possible."

"That's wonderful, Thompson. Are you drunk?"

"No, sir."

"Would you like to tell me, then, who was guarding that woman while you were out gallivanting all over the city?"

"I was. I'm marrying Hilary Campbell."

"You're marrying Ryan Jenkins's girlfriend?"

GRADY TOOK A HALF DAY OFF, which was just as well. He wasn't getting any work done anyway, so there wasn't much point in staying for the entire afternoon. As he left the station, he wondered whether Hilary's classes were through for the day. Almost simultaneously, it occurred to him that Stacy wouldn't be home until three-thirty. With those two thoughts in his mind, he turned the car toward the university.

When Grady got there, she wasn't in her office, so he checked with the departmental secretary, who told him Hilary had left with three men an hour earlier. Panic-stricken and fearing the worst, Grady demanded a description of the men. Once he got it, he sighed with relief and asked to use the telephone. A single phone call confirmed that she had indeed gone back to the firehouse with Michael and Paul, taking the plainclothes officer with her.

During the drive across town, Grady's annoyance heated up until, by the time he arrived at the firehouse, he was near the boiling point.

He was angry with Hilary for taking off without leaving word about where she was going. She was still in protective custody, after all—even if it wasn't like any other protective custody he'd ever seen before. He was angry with her two housemates for encouraging her. As far as he'd been able to tell, instigation was their chief function and reason for being. He was angry with the plainclothes officer for cooperating with the three partners in crime— the man should have had enough sense not to listen to that crew, not even for a minute.

As it turned out, however, the bait had been cheese-cake. Amaretto cheesecake, to be precise. The focus of

Grady's antagonism narrowed to Paul and then vaporized entirely when Paul offered him a piece.

Appeased by cheesecake, freshly-brewed coffee and the knowledge that Hilary was safe, Grady relaxed—so much so that he didn't notice the surreptitious looks her two housemates were exchanging. Hilary, however, caught them in the act and called them on it.

"Okay," she said, giving first one and then the other a level stare. "Give. What's going on here?"

Paul smiled innocently. It wouldn't have fooled her, even if Michael hadn't let the cat out of the bag. "Aw, Hilary, we meant well. And it turned out all right, after all."

"What did you do this time?" The words were spoken slowly and separately, as if she were forcibly restraining her temper until she heard the rest of it.

Michael fidgeted uneasily in his chair before continuing. "I know how upset you were when you couldn't find Ree," he told Grady. "But you didn't really have to worry about her."

"What are you talking about?" Grady asked. Every time he saw Hilary's two housemates, they made less and less sense. He consoled himself with the recognition that when they started to make sense, it would be time to worry about his own lucidity.

"Ree was never in any danger," Paul declared.

"*We* wrote the letter," Michael added.

"You were mad and Ree was mad and we didn't think—"

"You'd get back together on your own. But we thought that if you thought she was in danger, you'd come running—"

"Like a white knight or something."

"And you did."

Grady was stunned; he felt as if every ounce of air had been forced from his lungs. Hilary looked irked, embarrassed and resigned, all at the same time. The plainclothes officer just looked confused.

"Do you mean to tell me," Grady demanded, "that you filed a false police report that put Hilary in custody and tied me up investigating it for almost a week?"

"Right."

"Right."

The two answered simultaneously, and then Paul continued unrepentantly, "Look how well it turned out, though. The two of you got thrown together for a few days and got a chance to work things out."

Grady gave his head a vigorous shake to clear it, certain that doing so would make all this make sense. It did, unfortunately. "Do you have any idea what the penalty is for filing a false police report?"

"Charlie said—"

"Charlie told us—"

"Charlie was in on this?" Grady yelled, coming to his feet.

"Not from the beginning, exactly, but we talked to him when he came to pick up Hilary's stuff—"

"And he said he'd seen that memo about the vandalism on the cars in the parking lot—"

"Memo? What memo?"

"The one he threw away before you saw it," Michael said.

"And that's when we told him that we wrote the letter," Paul added.

"For God's sake, Charlie's a cop! He knows better!"

Michael grinned. "But he knew it'd work."

Grady was livid, but Hilary appeared mortified. "How could you do this to me? Never mind that— How could you do this to *Grady?*"

Paul shrugged. "It seemed like a good idea at the time."

"I've ruined his kitchen, his driveway, his grass—"

"Don't worry about the damned grass, Hilary!" Grady roared at her. "I told you it doesn't matter!"

When Grady started to yell at her instead of Paul and Michael, Hilary gulped, turned white, and looked as if she was going to cry.

Paul positively beamed at Michael. "See?"

Michael returned his satisfied nod. "Ain't love grand?"

"Damn it, Hilary! The plumber fixed it! And there wasn't any real damage from the fire!"

She edged even closer to tears.

"For God's sake, Hilary! What's it going to take to convince you that you're not going to drive me crazy?"

"He looks perfectly all right to me," Paul said to Michael.

Michael nodded.

The first traces of tears trickled down Hilary's face as she attempted to speak.

Grady saw her tears, stopped his tirade, and cursed under his breath as their cause became clear to him.

"Oh, baby, I'm sorry. . . ." He reached for her, enfolded her in his arms and cradled her head against his chest. Crooning softly, he held her until her sobbing slowed and finally stopped.

When she raised her head, her face glimmered with the last of her tears. His fingers gently stroked them from her cheeks as he asked, "You still don't believe me, do you, Hilary?"

She chewed nervously at her bottom lip until he put his hand to it and stopped her. His thumb soothed the impressions her teeth had left and, a moment later, he lowered his face to hers and covered them with his mouth. Drawing her abused lip into his mouth, he sucked on it. She moaned and shivered in response, tipping her head back to allow him greater access. He took full advantage of her offer.

They both forgot the attentive presence of Hilary's two roommates and the plainclothes officer, until Paul's voice filtered through their blissful haze.

"Now *that's* a kiss."

Abruptly, Grady's head jerked up, just as Hilary's turned around to glare at Paul. She sputtered at him furiously for a moment and then grabbed Grady's hand and dragged him from the room. Shortly afterward, the three men heard the front door slam.

Hilary sputtered and fumed most of the way back to Grady's house. Grady just fumed.

It was bad enough that Hilary's two housemates would engage in such nonsense, but Charlie's involvement in the scheme absolutely floored Grady. Although his partner had always made jokes about Grady being the sensible, reasonable, by-the-book one, Charlie had never given the slightest indication he'd participate in something so utterly unprofessional.

But he had.

And Grady had a sinking feeling that when he confronted Charlie with his knowledge of that collusion, he was going to get precisely the same answer from him that he'd gotten from Hilary's housemates: Guilty as charged, but it was for a good cause.

Because Hilary's nerves were still frayed from her crying spell earlier, Grady's lingering silence made her anxious, even as she continued to rail against her housemates' manipulation. She didn't have the slightest doubt that, as soon as they got back to the house, he was going to demand she pack her bags and return to the firehouse, where she belonged.

It was bad enough that Paul and Michael had conspired with Charlie in order to get her and Grady together; she didn't really blame them for that, because she knew they'd meant well. What infuriated her was the disastrous timing of their confession—*after* she and Grady had made love.

She screwed up relationships well enough on her own. God knew she didn't need any help in that department.

When they pulled into Grady's driveway, Hilary reached for the door handle even before the car came to a stop. It came off in her hand and she began to cry in frustration.

Grady put the car in neutral, set the brake, and shut it off before he spoke. "Lord, Hilary, I wish they hadn't done that."

She sniffed and hiccuped. "I...I..." she began, but gave up when the words wouldn't come out.

"Throwing us together to see what would happen, as if we were some sort of science project . . ."

She tried to speak again and failed.

"Bringing up those damned ex-fiancés every time we turned around . . ."

"I . . ."

"Hilary, I—"

"I'll get my stuff."

"I— What?" Grady's head whipped around and he stared at her, not understanding.

"I'll pack my things," she sniffed, resignation evident in her voice. "Go back home. Leave."

"But, Hilary—"

"You can't stand it anymore. I don't blame you, Grady. It's just the way I am."

"But—"

"You don't have to put up with it anymore. The kitchen, the driveway, the grass . . ."

"But—"

"The trips to West Virginia at three a.m., the—"

"But, Hilary—"

"I don't need a guard anymore. Actually, I guess I never did. I'm sorry about that. I didn't know Paul and Michael wrote the letter." She stuck out her hand, grabbed Grady's and began pumping it up and down. "Goodbye, Grady. Have a good life. No hard feelings. Keep in—"

As sharply as a bolt of lightning, Grady suddenly realized what Hilary thought. She actually believed he was going to break up with her, now that he'd learned there wasn't any need to guard her. Growling, he tightened his grip on her hand and yanked her toward him, into his arms. In spite of the gearshift wedged between them, his mouth sealed hers with a violent intensity that surpassed any of his previous kisses.

When he raised his head again, she was limp and trembling and breathless. She gaped at him wordlessly, her mouth still slightly open.

He took a deep breath in an effort to restrain himself from going after her again. It almost worked.

After another shattering kiss, he leaned his head back against his own seat to try again—he had to convince her that she had been completely wrong.

"Do you really believe I'd rather have healthy grass than that?" he demanded. "What do you think I am, Hilary? Nuts?"

She shook her head, still unable to speak.

"No more talk about going back to the firehouse, okay?"

Her head bobbed up and down rapidly.

"*Now*, do you believe I really want to marry you?"

She nodded again. "Does this mean we're engaged?"

He detected a hint of panic in her voice and rushed to head it off before it turned into another onslaught. "No. Like I said before, Hilary... I don't want to be your fiancé."

"Oh."

"Now, come on. Let's go into the house." He got out of the car, walked around to open her door, and helped her out after prying the detached door handle from her fingers.

"Can I cook supper?" she asked hopefully.

"I love you, sweetheart, but don't push it."

When they entered the house, he was profoundly relieved and grateful that Stacy had already begun dinner preparations.

CHARLIE DID NOT TRY to deny his complicity in the deception. On the other hand, he made it quite clear that he was prepared to renounce every word of his confession if Grady mentioned it to Lieutenant Angelucci, who would undoubtedly go right through the ceiling if he found out.

"Aw, Grady, come on," Charlie coaxed when Grady balked at his suggestion that they ought to come up with another story, purely for the lieutenant's benefit. They both knew they had to tell him something, in order to justify removing all mention of the threat from the case file. "You wouldn't want us both to end up on report for this, would you?"

"Both of us?" Grady disputed, but with no real heat. Just because he was going to give in to Charlie eventually, that didn't mean he intended to make it easy for him. "Hey, I'm as innocent as a babe in all this."

"Yeah, but you were the beneficiary, not me. And we're partners, aren't we? It's like blood brothers, except messier," Charlie reasoned. "Besides that, we're on the phone, with no corroborating witnesses. Anything you tell him would only be hearsay."

"Now, Charlie—"

"Inadmissible evidence."

"You can't expect me to lie—"

"You didn't Mirandize me—that pair at the firehouse, either, I bet."

"—to the lieutenant."

"It's a bad bust, but Angelucci'll probably want to press charges against them for filing a false report."

Grady sighed. "So what're we gonna tell him, then?"

"That it was just a misunderstanding?" Charlie suggested.

"A misunderstanding?" Grady echoed skeptically. It sounded pretty flimsy to him.

By the time they hung up their respective telephones ten minutes later, they'd agreed to tell Angelucci that they'd learned that one of Hilary's students had been angry about a bad grade, made the threat in the heat of the moment and hadn't been serious about it. While it put a substantial dent in what both of them knew to be the truth, they agreed that no harm would be done by the deception. The lieutenant would undoubtedly agree that it would serve no real purpose to press charges against a college freshman who wasn't guilty of anything more than youthful excitability and poor judgment. He wouldn't be as lenient with two full-grown adults and a police detective, all of whom knew better and had done it intentionally.

Not long after Grady and Charlie offered that explanation, word came back down that the powers-that-be wanted the Ryan Jenkins case resolved ASAP—yesterday wasn't soon enough to suit them.

The pressure from above made Lieutenant Angelucci cranky, so neither Grady nor Charlie pointed out the obvious: that they'd been working on this case all along, and hadn't made any headway on it yet. All leads had led to the same place—straight into a dead-end alley.

Thus far, they'd systematically investigated and eliminated from consideration the second- and third-string players competing for Jenkins's position, a handful of walk-on wanna-bees who had been cut during training camp, a few not-very-serious ex-girlfriends, the coach of the team Jenkins had played for prior to being signed by the Titans, and a couple of Pittsburgh's most prominent bookies. Not only did none of them seem to have a recent unexplained infusion of cash—except for the bookies, *all* of whose cash was unexplained—none of them appeared to harbor the degree of animosity—or information—that would suggest extortion. As far as they could tell during the interviews they'd conducted, everyone seemed to like and respect Ryan Jenkins, and no one knew anything bad about him.

"He can't be as much of a saint as everyone keeps saying," Charlie groused as they left yet another unproductive interview a few mornings later. "He *has* to have done something to get someone mad at him."

"Not only that," Grady added, "he has to have done something bad enough to get blackmailed for. We didn't even find a traffic ticket for him when we ran a check on him."

"What's Hilary say about it?"

"Hilary? Hilary says *nothing*—not a single word—on the subject of Ryan Jenkins."

Misinterpreting the edge in Grady's voice for jealousy and continued doubts about Hilary's relationship with Jenkins, Charlie asked, "You don't still think that Hilary and Jenkins—"

"Lord, no!" Grady interrupted. In spite of the fact that her refusal to discuss Ryan Jenkins's blackmail case had caused some minor turbulence between them, he didn't believe for a minute that there had ever been anything between the two of them but friendship. Hilary had told him so, and he believed her. He just wished she'd tell him everything she knew, and be done with it. "But she knows something, and she won't tell me. I can see it in her eyes."

"You want me to try?"

Grady shook his head, settled in behind the wheel of the K-Car, and slid the key into the ignition. "Trust me on this one. She isn't gonna tell you, either. We're more likely to get Jenkins to tell us the truth himself."

"Terrific." They'd both been frustrated by the interview they'd finally gotten when they'd caught up with Jenkins between away games. It had been as futile as all the rest. They got the distinct impression the man simply didn't want to tell them what they needed to know to solve the case. "Wanna call it a morning and head for lunch before we go and talk to him again?"

As Grady started the engine and put the car into gear, Charlie commented, "Things are going pretty well with Hilary, I take it? It looks like she's moved in for good."

"It does, doesn't it?"

Grady grinned, in spite of the fact that his house was starting to look like the back of the Mazda, now that Hilary was living there in every way but officially. He figured he'd take care of that in good time. For now, it was enough that she'd stayed even after they'd learned that she wasn't in any danger. One piece at a time, her belongings had made the trip over from the firehouse. It wasn't quite what he was used to, but he liked seeing her clutter strewn around his house as if it—and she—belonged. If he had to wade through an endless ocean of shoes to get out of his own bedroom or conduct a full-house search for the pliers Hilary had misplaced—again—well, those were just small prices to pay.

In response to the discovery that his house just wasn't as big as he'd thought it was, Grady was giving serious consideration to having the attic finished for additional living space. Paul and Michael had known what they were doing when they'd dedicated the entire third floor of the firehouse to her use.

He gave Hilary cooking lessons, which forced him to replace his toaster, a nonstick skillet, and several assorted small plastic utensils that were casualties of her efforts. Resignedly, he bought a fire extinguisher and signed a service contract for the garbage disposal.

The telephone was perpetually busy, as much as if he had two teenagers in the house instead of one. After spending more than an hour trying to call his own house, he'd finally, in desperation, called the firehouse, gotten the number for Hilary's answering service from Paul, called there, and had her paged. Immediately after she returned his call, he'd had "call waiting" added to his telephone service.

As far as Grady was concerned, all of these things were negligible. Hilary's presence in his bed and what happened between them there vastly overcompensated for whatever happened out of it. Every time disaster struck, as it inevitably did, the reminder that one-third of a person's life is spent in bed was one of the things that kept his sanity intact.

It wasn't that his relationship with Hilary was based solely on great sex; it was much more than that. The same passion and vitality she brought to his bedroom, she brought to the rest of his life. He hadn't realized, before meeting her, just how boring and regimented and sterile his life had become. Even the chaos that followed her like the agitated wake of a ship reminded him that he was alive, in a peculiar sort of way.

Being a sensible man, Grady was not entirely oblivious to the implications of either of those reflections. The specter of male menopause had, in fact, raised its ugly head right at the beginning. He hadn't revealed his misgivings to anyone, not even to Charlie, who would have laughed; or to Hilary, who already had enough doubts of her own, without his contributions. Since then, he had read numerous magazine articles on the subject. After having given methodical consideration to the possibility that his attraction to Hilary was rooted in a fear of turning forty and a desire to recapture his youth with a younger woman, he rejected the idea outright. It just didn't fit.

After thinking things through, he'd concluded that Hilary's age wasn't really an issue, at least not to him. She wasn't a naive little girl looking for a daddy to take care of her, as many of the younger women those articles talked about seemed to be. She was feisty and independent and worldly-wise in a way many women his own age were not. She knew and accepted without question people and things that made him, a veteran police detective, pause. And if she was a little squirrelly... well, he suspected she would probably still be squirrelly when she was fifty-six. Or seventy-six. Or a hundred and six. She wouldn't be Hilary if she weren't.

The difference in their ages didn't appear to matter to Hilary, either. She didn't even notice it, as far as he could tell. In the time he'd known her, he'd observed her with other people and she seemed utterly oblivious to the matter of age, not only with him, but with everyone. Her friends ranged in age from twenty to sixty and she treated the differences with complete disregard. Even her two housemates were far closer in age to him than they were to her; Paul, Grady knew, was the same age he was, and Michael was about thirty-five.

All that aside, the only thing that really mattered was that Grady loved Hilary with every fiber of his being and couldn't begin to imagine spending the rest of his life without her. He'd never expected to fall like this after losing Anne. Marriage to Hilary wasn't going to be calm, as his marriage to Anne had been; but if he wanted it—and he did—he was going to have to deal with everything that came with it, including weirdo friends, constant uproar, and thirty pairs of shoes.

HILARY HAD ENTIRELY too many concerns of her own to give much thought to the issue of age difference. In spite of the current lull, she was convinced it was just a matter of time before Grady lost his temper, just like the others, and asked her to move out. It was inevitable—like tides and phases of the moon and lost car keys.

She worried about the way her things were taking over his house and resolved to be neater. Although she recognized that confining thirty pairs of shoes to the bedroom was not exactly solving the problem, she did her best to keep them from taking over the rest of the house.

Hilary made every effort to learn what Grady tried to teach her about cooking, and even made covert trips to the firehouse for remedial lessons from Paul. Her attempts were marginally successful, since she actually learned to cook three or four relatively edible meals. In the process, however, she was systematically destroying not one, but two kitchens, one of which was Paul's pride and joy. She began to worry that she wouldn't have a place to move when Grady asked her to leave.

She took note of Grady's annoyance with the telephone situation and offered to pay for the call waiting. Although he refused, she slipped the money for its installation and the first three months into his wallet while he wasn't looking.

In spite of his insistence that the oil spill didn't matter, Hilary scrubbed the spot in the driveway with degreaser and got out most of the stain. She then tore a clump of grass from an inconspicuous place in the yard, took it to a nursery, explained about the oil spill, and asked them how to fix it. Horrified, she handed over thirty-two dollars for a bag of grass seed and something they told her would neutralize the oil in the soil. She was extremely relieved when it appeared to work, though Grady never actually commented on it.

There were times Hilary couldn't help noticing the veins that stood out on Grady's neck and a slight twitch by his right eye that made her nervous, mostly because she remembered that same twitch from Kevin, fiancé number five. She didn't have to be told that both mannerisms revealed the tension that Grady resolutely denied. The only time he completely relaxed, as far as she could tell, was when they were in bed. It made sense, at least to her, because it was probably the only time he could be relatively certain what was going to happen next.

At first, she had worried that Grady's attraction to her was nothing more than sexual. As an indirect result of her security in that single aspect of their relationship, she made a clean sweep of Kaufmann's lingerie department Tuesday afternoon. When he saw the colorful heap of silk and lace that night, he intuitively sensed the motivation behind it and assured her she was wrong. His argument was so persuasive, she returned half of it Wednesday morning.

It all came back to Grady's repeated assertions that he intended to marry her. According to Grady, Hilary was the only woman he'd considered marrying since Anne's death. He'd been happily married for twelve years, after all, and knew what marriage was about. He'd been widowed for five years since then, which had given him plenty of time to locate a suitable wife, if that was all he wanted. His absolute certainty about marrying her told Hilary that Grady's feelings for her went far beyond mere desire. Hers certainly did. As much as Grady wanted her to be his wife, she wanted him to be her husband. Maybe more so.

Hilary's biggest fear wasn't the thought of being married to Grady; she was pretty sure she could handle that, if she didn't make him crazy. Beyond that, though, she wasn't operating entirely on solid ground. Marriage, home and family all went together in his mind, she was sure, and she was absolutely terrified that he hadn't been exactly truthful when he'd told her it was up to her whether or not they had more children. Seeing him with Stacy assured her that he'd want more, and she wasn't really certain she was mother material. She liked other people's children well enough, but she also liked the fact that she could give them back to their owners when she was through with them.

Even as she began to acknowledge that Grady just might be the man to put the madness aside and love her enough to marry her, she made no immediate plans to stop taking her birth-control pills.

She did, however, feel confident enough to agree to Paul's proposal for a non-engagement party for her and Grady.

# 9

THURSDAY NIGHT, HILARY stood in front of her closet back at the firehouse, made a complete inventory of its bulging contents, and decided she didn't have a thing to wear for the party the following night. Nothing suitable, at any rate. Except for the cheongsam her mother had sent her, her only really dressy clothes were the ones she'd bought for her hostessing job, and all of those were much too glitzy; for that matter, the Chinese dress was, too. And the dresses she'd gotten to satisfy the fiancés' ideas of what she ought to wear for dress-up were out of the question. In addition to evoking bad memories, every last one made her look like a Baptist minister's wife. And her everyday clothes—Laura Ashley, the Tina Turner look, Miss Preppy or the fifties debutante—just weren't festive enough.

What she really wanted was something gala, but subtle. If it were Christmas, she would have gone for plaid taffeta. If it were summer, the Scarlett O'Hara look.

Shrugging her shoulders, she finally told herself she had to go shopping for something new to wear. She fished through her dresser drawers, collected a formidable assortment of underwear that would accommodate virtually anything she might buy, and tossed it into a shopping bag. She didn't worry about shoes, because they were all at Grady's house already.

She lugged the bag down to the first floor, where Grady was waiting for her. She hadn't been sure it was wise to leave him alone with Paul and Michael long enough to go upstairs and pick out clothes, but Paul's apple dumplings, still hot from the oven, had been too good an offer for Grady to resist.

Her worst fears were confirmed even before Hilary got to the kitchen door. Carrying clearly into the living room was their description of the last time she had come home in disgrace, after Jack, fiancé number seven, had broken *that* engagement. It had been a particularly ugly scene, even for her.

She and Jack had been at a dinner party with his boss when the waiter had come over to the table and told them there was an emergency call for Jack. The emergency, it turned out, was a flood in Jack's condo building, affecting not only his unit, but the one directly below it. The source of the flood was Jack's dishwasher, which Hilary had loaded and started before they'd left for dinner.

"So, then," Hilary heard Michael say in a voice that was entirely too gleeful to suit her, "Jack stood there and started screaming at Ree in front of his boss and everybody. He called her every name in the book and a few he invented just for the occasion. She started crying and his boss's wife—"

"Who does volunteer work with abused women, came to Ree's defense," Paul interrupted. "She wanted to call the cops before Jack hit her or something—"

"Which he wouldn't have done, because Jack really wasn't like that. By the time it was all over, Jack almost got fired, because his boss's wife was convinced he was some sort of woman abuser."

"Jack started blaming her for that, too, and the next thing she knew, he'd broken off the engagement."

"Ree straightened it all out later. So, of course, he didn't get fired, and it turned out the dishwasher's hose was plugged up and the flood wasn't really her fault, anyway."

In the living room, Hilary cringed, wondering what her two housemates thought they were doing, and tried to decide whether to break in on their performance or just leave without Grady. *Perhaps for Australia* came to mind.

"Did she at least get an apology from this jerk?" she heard Grady say. She smiled gratefully. It sounded as if he was angry at Jack on her behalf, instead of empathizing with him.

"Later," Michael answered. "But it was too late for them to get back together again."

"Just as well," Paul added. "Jack was never right for her, anyway."

Before Paul went any further, Hilary thought it was time to make her entrance. She made lots of noise in the living room to give them fair warning. Why she felt an obligation to be fair to either of them was an unsolved mystery—neither was exactly being fair to her.

AFTER COLLECTING HER bag of underwear and three of the apple dumplings, she and Grady returned to his house in the T-bird, which had just been returned from the body shop that afternoon. A note on the table from Stacy informed them that she was at Julie's and reminded Grady that classes at her school would be dismissed at noon the following day.

"Do you think she'd want to go shopping with me?" Hilary asked after reading the note.

"She's a high school girl," Grady answered matter-of-factly. "Of course, she'd like to go shopping. The girl lives to shop."

"I'll ask her when she gets home."

"It says here she'll be back about ten." Grady looked at his watch. "It's seven now."

"That gives us three hours to eat all the dumplings before she gets back."

"Wrong." Grady grinned meaningfully, slipped his arm around her waist, and lowered his head to nuzzle at her nape. "That gives us three hours to be alone before she comes back."

AT NOON THE FOLLOWING morning, Hilary carefully moved the Thunderbird, which had been blocking the Mazda, went to pick up Stacy at school and drove to the Monroeville Mall, located in the suburbs. During a two-hour race through the huge, two-level mall, they had eaten lunch, purchased a new tie and matching socks for Grady, had make-overs done at the department-store cosmetics department, and gotten Stacy's ears pierced. They had not, however, found a dress special enough for Hilary to wear to the party that evening.

On their way back to Grady's house in Highland Park, they elected to stop in Shadyside. Though Hilary had known she would find something appropriate at one of the shops there, she'd saved it as a last resort, because most of the stores were expensive. Very expensive.

Hilary was right; she found exactly what she'd had in mind, although she didn't know it until she saw it. She and Stacy both loved the dress, which made her look and feel like a Renaissance princess. Made of a deep royal blue satin that rustled when she moved, it had a fitted bodice with a square neckline, huge gathered elbow-length sleeves, a tea-length skirt so full it billowed around her when she sat, and a black-and-blue brocade sash with a big bow at the back. Its price made the teddy and comb coat seem positively reasonable.

It was a foregone conclusion that Hilary would buy the dress anyway. She practically had to force herself to take it off so the saleswoman could put it in its garment bag. And before she'd even paid for it, Stacy asked if she could borrow it for the Christmas dance, which was more than seven months away.

Hilary looked at Stacy consideringly and chewed her bottom lip. In spite of the dress's basically modest cut, it was impossible to wear a bra of any type under it because of the broad, square neckline; additionally, its sewn-in crinoline eliminated the need for a slip and generated static with even the mere addition of panties. She strongly suspected Grady was going to have vehement objections to Stacy wearing a dress with nothing underneath it but panties and hose.

"We'll see," Hilary finally answered, reluctant to explain further.

When they got back to the house, Hilary saw immediately that Grady hadn't come home yet and the Thunderbird was right where she'd left it—in the middle of the driveway and in the way. After putting the Mazda into neutral and setting the brake, she dug in her purse for Grady's keys and then reached for the door handle.

"I'll do it," Stacy offered.

"Pull in the Mazda? You can drive a standard?"

"No," Stacy admitted. "But Daddy's car's an automatic. I can move it over to give you room."

Hilary thought about it. "Have you ever done this before?"

Stacy nodded. "He lets me, but only in the driveway."

Hilary hesitated for a moment before handing the keys to Stacy. "All right. But be careful."

"I will." Stacy got out of the Mazda, walked over to the Thunderbird and got in.

As Hilary watched from her own car, Stacy started the engine and cautiously moved the vintage automobile to one side of the driveway. When she stopped, Hilary pulled in beside her, turned off her own car, opened her door and started to get out. She had one foot on the ground when the Thunderbird suddenly lurched backward, off the driveway, across the newly-sprouted grass, over two small shrubs and into the corner of the house.

Leaving her car door standing open, Hilary dropped her purse and the new dress, ran across the driveway to the Thunderbird and yanked open its driver's door. "Stacy? Are you all right?"

Stacy looked up at her and nodded, although she winced. "Daddy's car!" she wailed.

"Don't worry about the car. Are *you* all right?" Hilary demanded.

"I'm fine—for now, at least. But when Daddy sees his car . . ."

"Did that used to be a Thunderbird?" a deep voice behind Hilary asked. She spun around and saw Zeke Murdough standing there. He'd dropped by unexpectedly and had arrived just in time to witness the tragedy. "A 1964 Thunderbird?"

Hilary and Stacy both nodded wordlessly.

"The same Thunderbird Grady was driving the day he met you?" he asked Hilary.

Again, Hilary and Stacy nodded.

With a grave expression on his face, Zeke walked around to the back of the car and looked at the damages to both the car and the house. Finally, he spoke. "Could've been worse."

"Can we get it fixed in—" Hilary looked at her watch. "—an hour and a half?"

Zeke shook his head. "Not a chance. I don't even think two hours would cover it."

All three of them sighed.

"Let's put it in the garage," Stacy suggested. "He won't see it until tomorrow."

Hilary and Zeke glanced at each other and considered the idea. It had its merits, chief among them that Hilary could confess before Grady discovered it on his own. She and Zeke nodded simultaneously.

IF TWO HOURS WOULD have been enough time to repair the car, they could have done it, because Grady was late returning from the station. He and Charlie had been held up working on the Connors case, which they'd believed was closed—until that afternoon. Though Connors been found guilty by a jury of his peers, his lawyers had filed an appeal, charging that there had been procedural errors that warranted a retrial. The prosecutor's office had been very upset about the allegations and had insisted on having a full report by the following morning, so Charlie and Grady had spent the remainder of the day going through and documenting every item in the file. It had been a long, arduous process, but, in the end, they thought they'd proved that they hadn't dropped the ball.

As he pulled into the driveway and parked next to the Mazda, Grady hoped Stacy and Hilary were ready to go to the party at the firehouse, allowing him sole occupancy of at least one of the bathrooms. Otherwise, they were never going to make it.

He got out of the K-Car and reached into the back seat for his suit, fresh from the cleaners. When he raised his head, the first thing he saw was the skid mark on the new grass, making him forget all about the Connors case and his tiredness. His eyes followed its trail across the yard, over the two smashed shrubs, to the corner of the house—or what used to be a corner; it was sort of rounded now.

He spun around and eyed the Mazda behind him suspiciously. Slowly he walked around the car, checking all four corners for incriminating evidence. There wasn't any. The car didn't have a scratch on it anywhere. An eerie premonition, almost a sense of déjà vu, crept over him. The last time the Mazda had sat untouched amid the wreckage, the Thunderbird had been smashed. He had left it in the driveway that morning, but it wasn't there now.

After taking a deep, steadying breath, Grady walked to the garage and raised the door. He groaned heavily when he saw the damage to the classic automobile. The house had gotten the best of it in their confrontation. For that matter, so had the grass and shrubs. He closed his eyes and counted slowly to ten. He told himself it was only a car, an inanimate assembly of metal and glass. He reminded himself that such disasters had been the end of every one of Hilary's relationships thus far and he was determined not to let that happen to this one.

At last, his temper reined in—or so he hoped—he lowered the garage door and walked over to the house.

As he opened the atrium door, he heard Zeke Murdough's voice speak. "It's really nice, isn't it? They don't carry it in the Pennsylvania liquor stores."

Grady stopped uncomfortably and closed the atrium door quietly behind him.

"Maybe there isn't a market for a wine in this price range," he heard Hilary answer.

"You know better than that, Ree. Even if I asked twenty-five hundred a case, I'd get it. This is the only case I haven't sold, because I'm keeping it for myself."

"Greedy," Hilary accused.

"If I were greedy, I wouldn't be sharing it with you two, would I? What do you think of it, Stacy?"

Stacy? Stacy? Grady's jaw clenched, he dropped his suit to the floor, and stepped into the doorway of the family room. Between Stacy and Hilary, both dressed for the party, sat Zeke Murdough, liquor-and-cigarette smuggler. On the table in front of the sectional was a bottle of wine, and all three of them had wineglasses. As he watched speechlessly, Stacy took a sip from her glass.

"I don't know," she said, making a face. "I think it's kind of sour."

"That's body, Stacy," Zeke told her. "Wine's not supposed to be sweet."

None of the three people seated on the sectional noticed Grady until he roared—suddenly, wordlessly and violently. When he did, all three of them looked up at him and gasped.

Finally, he forced out real words. "How *dare* you?"

"We were just..." Hilary began, her face pale and frightened.

"I can see what you were doing! What were you thinking, Hilary? Giving her liquor?"

"One glass of—"

"I can see what it is! She's just a kid! Are you out of your mind?"

"We—"

"But Hilary was just—" Stacy offered.

"You—don't say anything, young lady! Go to your room!" He glared at his daughter and saw something glint beneath her hair, which was pulled back, away from her face. "What the hell did you do to your ears?"

She gulped. "Got them pierced," she finally admitted. Then she fled.

Grady turned back to Hilary, ignoring Zeke. "What's wrong with you, Hilary? You're supposed to be the grown-up here! Not her conspirator! Or worse..."

Hilary turned even more ashen and didn't speak. Tears welled up in her eyes, and she struggled to blink them back.

"Smashing the Thunderbird into the house wasn't enough, was it?"

Hilary fought back the tears, trembling as she did so.

"All right, Hilary, I give up! I surrender! Enough is enough! Don't you have any sense at all? Do you do this deliberately? Were you trying to prove me wrong? Prove you could drive me just as crazy as the rest of them? It worked! You've proved to me, beyond a shadow of a doubt, that you're a menace to my mental health!"

With that, Hilary jumped up from the sectional and ran out the back door. In the silence she left behind, both men heard the Mazda start, back out of the driveway, and peel away down the street.

WHEN HILARY RAN INTO the living room of the firehouse a short time later, Michael and Ryan Jenkins were moving furniture in preparation for the party. Both men took one look at the expression on her face, recognized it immediately, and put down their respective ends of the sofa.

"Paul!" Ryan yelled, as Michael grabbed Hilary's arms and forced her to sit on the sofa. "Get out here! Now!"

"But I'm in the middle of . . ." Paul's answer carried in from the kitchen.

"Now!"

Paul rushed through the door and stopped abruptly when he saw Hilary sitting beside Michael. She was hyperventilating, and Michael was encouraging her to breathe normally.

"Damn," Paul muttered. "I thought he was gonna be the one to make it."

"Apparently not," Ryan commented.

Paul went to the sofa and sat on the other side of Hilary, across from Michael. "What happened this time, honey?"

"Car—" Hilary forced out between gasps. "Stacy— ears—"

Paul and Michael exchanged glances over her head and sighed.

"Zeke—"

Paul turned to Ryan. "Can you finish putting the nuts on top of the Brie?"

Ryan nodded and retreated to the kitchen.

"C'mon, Ree. Breathe," Michael told her as he rubbed circles on her back. "In. Out. You can do it."

Hilary's breathing finally returned to normal, and Paul asked again, "Can you tell us what happened?"

The whole story tumbled out, beginning with Stacy and Hilary's trip to the mall and ending with Hilary's flight from Grady's house. As she told it, Paul and Michael both nodded understandingly. When she finished, Paul observed evenly, "By the way, I love the dress."

She looked down at herself and her bottom lip quivered threateningly. "So did I. Shadyside."

"I know." Paul sighed again. "So, what happens now?"

Hilary shook her head sadly. "Can we call off the party?"

Michael looked down at his watch and then shook his head. "Too late for that."

Paul thought for a moment. "Look, we never said it was an engagement party—"

"It wasn't," Hilary sniffed. "Grady said . . . said . . ."

"I know, honey." Paul patted her shoulder consolingly. "What I was thinking was, we could just say the party was for something else."

Michael's head shot up and he snapped his fingers as he remembered. "Your Paris voucher came today."

Paul beamed and nodded. "That's it. This can be a farewell party for Hilary before her trip to Paris!"

"But . . ." She tried to tell them she wasn't going to Paris until after the semester ended, but they interrupted her.

"That's just a technicality," Paul pointed out.

"Hilary," Michael asked, "do you think you can carry this off?"

Before she could reply, Paul assured their housemate, "Of course, she can. It's not as if she hasn't done it before. Now, go on upstairs and fix your face before they get here."

AFTER HILARY'S DEPARTURE Grady sank down onto the sectional and swore profoundly.

"I guess that about sums it up," Zeke remarked dolefully.

"Why did I do that?" Grady asked. The question really wasn't addressed to Zeke, but he answered it anyway.

"A loose connection between your brain and your mouth?"

"I promised myself I wasn't going to do that." Grady reached for one of the glasses on the table and drained it without thinking. "No matter what she did."

Zeke winced as he watched the liquid disappear but kept silent.

Grady reached for another glass and drained it, too—still without a moment's consideration. "I lost it."

Zeke nodded in silent agreement, eyeing the rest of the wine in the bottle.

"I shouldn't have lost my temper," Grady continued. "I should have been able to reason with her. Calmly, adult to adult."

Zeke finally spoke: "The Thunderbird wasn't her fault. Stacy moved it out of Hilary's way so she could pull into the driveway. She said you'd let her do it before."

Grady nodded in confirmation.

"When she finished moving it, she put it into reverse instead of park."

"When I saw the house and the Thunderbird, I was fine. Well, not fine, exactly, but I had it together. And then I came in here and you...and Stacy...and the wine...and the ears...." Grady's hands flailed for a moment and he reached for the third glass.

Zeke spoke up. "You're not a wine buff, are you?"

Grady shook his head. "This isn't bad, though."

Zeke sighed in resignation. "*This* is a 1983 Château d'Yquem. It can't be bought in Pennsylvania, except by special order. In Maryland, it's over a thousand dollars a case. By the time Pennsylvania's liquor board gets hold of it, it's almost three thousand dollars a case."

Grady mentally divided that by twelve bottles in a case and choked on the bit of wine that was still in his mouth.

"Now, you're a cop and I shouldn't tell you this—"

Grady shook his head. "I won't say anything."

"But I just brought in fifty cases of it. It's all sold, except for one case I'm keeping. I brought over a bottle so you and Hilary could try it."

Grady looked silently at Zeke. It had been an extremely generous gesture, which he appreciated in spite of its illegality.

"You weren't here, but we opened it anyway."

"But why—"

"Did we give Stacy a glass?" Zeke finished for Grady. "Did you know Hilary's family had lived in France?"

Grady shook his head again. If he lived to be a hundred, he'd still be learning things about her. Assuming, of course, that she was still somewhere in the general vicinity. At the moment, the odds of that happening didn't look good. "No. I know they're somewhere in Asia now, but—"

"Taiwan," Zeke provided. "Before that, her dad was in charge of Easterbrook's offices in Paris, so they lived there, in a country where they give small children glasses of wine mixed with water with their meals. By the time they're Stacy's age, they're drinking straight wine."

"I've heard that before."

"Hilary's used to seeing wine in a family atmosphere. Everybody gets a glass." Zeke peered at Grady. "It's basically a healthy attitude, because it gets rid of the mystique and fascination kids have about drinking."

Grady looked down at the wineglass he was turning in his hands, but didn't speak.

"I don't have a daughter, Thompson, but I know that if I did, I'd sure rather her first drink was in my house, where she was safe with Hilary and me, than have her be in a car with some seventeen-year-old guy with more hormones than brains."

Zeke's words generated a vivid picture of Brandon Pengelly in Grady's mind, and he shuddered at the image.

"Ree told me what happened last Friday night after you two left the club."

Grady's head shot up and he stared at Zeke. Surely she hadn't told him about what had happened on their way home. She wouldn't . . .

"Stacy's growing up," Zeke continued, and Grady exhaled, relieved that Hilary had only told Zeke about the incident with Stacy and Brandon after they had gotten home. "She's a good kid, Thompson. Don't get me wrong, but she's fifteen. Fifteen-year-olds aren't noted for their common sense."

"Neither is Hilary," Grady thought, unaware that he said it aloud until Zeke disputed it.

"That's not really true, Thompson. For the last three years, while she was a full-time student and taught classes, she ran her own business."

"Working as a hostess."

"Thompson, she didn't just show up in pretty dresses and greet people at the door." Grady's surprised expression prompted him to clarify himself in a voice that reeked of impatience. "No, not that. She organized everything for those parties—caterers, waiters, bartenders, table settings, seating arrangements, flowers—everything, sometimes for as many as a thousand people. The only reason she quit now was that she's getting into the home stretch on her dissertation and she doesn't have time to do it anymore."

"Oh." Grady felt stupid and guilty—both at the same time—and was painfully aware that both feelings were justified.

"That's an awful lot to ask from a woman with no common sense, isn't it?"

Grady nodded reluctantly.

"She's been an equal partner in the mortgage payments on the firehouse for three years, so you can't really say she doesn't have a sense of responsibility, either, can you?"

Grady shook his head and winced.

"And she's got street-smarts and loyalty and integrity. More than anyone I know. Think about the way she hauled that kid out of here last Friday. Bailed me and Manny out of jail. Covered for Ryan and Paul."

Grady's jaw dropped and he croaked, "Ryan and Paul?"

Zeke nodded calmly. "She didn't tell you? I'm not surprised. Not a lot of people know about it."

Everything began to make sense to Grady. The blackmailers. Hilary's assertion that it wasn't her secret to tell. He finally knew what Ryan Jenkins's deep, dark secret was.

"If it ever went public, it would ruin Ryan's career. His image and the endorsements would go right down the tubes. As long as everyone believed he and Hilary were lovers, he didn't have to worry about anyone connecting him with someone else—someone he couldn't acknowledge. Everything was just fine, until Marshall figured out who Paul was with now, and decided to use the information to see if he could get Paul back again."

The telephone rang, but both men ignored it.

"Marshall?" Grady remembered where he'd heard that name, all too vividly. "Paul's ex-lover?"

"The same one. He's smart enough to know that Ryan can't afford to let you prosecute him, because he'll tell."

The telephone's ringing stopped abruptly, mid-ring.

Zeke smiled ferally. "Fortunately, he's also smart enough to appreciate that certain friends of mine, who just found out what he was doing and had a long talk with him, really don't care about things like due process."

This, Grady didn't want to know about.

"You know, Thompson, right up until you charged in here bellowing like a wounded moose, I thought you were better than the others, that you'd be able to see past the nonsense to what Hilary really is inside."

Grady groaned and his head dropped back against the top of the sectional. "I'm such an ass," he muttered.

"Won't get any argument from me," Zeke bluntly told him.

Grady raised his head and turned to look at Zeke. "You've known her a long time...." Zeke nodded and Grady continued. "Do you think if I went and groveled, she'd come back?"

"I don't know, Thompson," Zeke answered honestly. "You said some awful things to her."

"I know," Grady admitted. "I'd give anything to take them back. Zeke, I'm not the kind of guy that blows up like that. I never did until I met Hilary."

"And you want to keep doing it?" Zeke gaped at him incredulously. "Never mind, it's *your* blood pressure."

At that moment, Stacy poked her head into the room timidly, as if gauging the atmosphere there before she committed herself to entering. "Daddy?"

Grady looked up at her. "Yes, Stacy?"

"Paul was just on the phone. The one that lives with Hilary," she reminded him needlessly.

"And?" He hadn't the slightest doubt that Paul had called to read him the riot act for hurting Hilary, and he wondered how extensively Paul had expanded Stacy's vocabulary.

"He says the university sent the voucher for Hilary to go to Paris and she's called and made reservations."

Grady went absolutely white. She'd told him about tutoring and the voucher, but it had never occurred to him that she might use it immediately. Actually, he'd thought they could both go there together on their honeymoon.

"He says she's packing," Stacy added.

Grady took a deep breath and cursed. "What am I going to do now?" he demanded of Zeke. "I was going to give her some time to calm down first, but if she goes to Paris—"

"Get dressed."

"What?"

"Go put on that suit you just carried in here and let's get going."

HILARY HAD NEVER BEEN in less of a mood to go to a party, but she really didn't have much choice in the matter. As Paul and Michael reminded her, it was much too late to call the guests and tell them not to come. The kitchen was overflowing with food, everything from canapés and cheeses to éclairs. She was already wearing a gorgeous, expensive, nonreturnable dress. According to her housemates, all she had to do was repair the damage to her makeup, calm down, and pray she could pull this one off when she went back downstairs to greet her guests.

Her makeup was the easiest part of it, because everything she had purchased from the make-over that afternoon was still out in her car. The rest of her mission sounded nothing short of impossible.

Alone, up in her bedroom, she regretted that her sure-fire method for composing herself—a long, hot bubble bath—was out of the question. Being dressed was the only thing she had under control at the moment, and it seemed pointless to ruin it. She did, however, put on her headphones to block out everything but Debussy, close her eyes, and try the meditation exercises she had learned from Michael.

They helped—a little.

Hilary told herself firmly that she had been through this seven times already and, by this point, should be an old hand at keeping up a brave front after being dumped. The only thing that reminder accomplished was to make her even more depressed than she already was.

It wasn't fair, she thought. Other people had perfectly normal relationships. They met someone, fell in love and got married. She, on the other hand, met someone, fell in love and got burned. Not burned, she corrected herself. With Grady, she had been fried to a crisp.

She never should have let it get as far as it had. It would have been so much better for both of them if she had just let him continue to believe she and Ryan were lovers. If she had any sense at all, she'd go out and get Property of Ryan Jenkins tattooed across her forehead so she never, ever, had to deal with this kind of heartbreak again. First thing in the morning, she would have to look into the matter. Meanwhile, there was still the party to get through.

After a last deep breath to brace herself for the ordeal she knew the party was going to be, she removed the headphones, brushed her hair, and headed for the spiral stairs, grimly assuring herself that any resemblance between this walk and Marie-Antoinette's trip to the Place de la Concorde was merely coincidence.

GRADY SWORE AND SLAMMED his fist on the dash of the K-Car, which was stopped because of a huge accident that had brought traffic on Forbes Avenue to a complete halt.

"If you keep it up, Thompson, either your hand or the dash is gonna get broken. It doesn't matter to me, because neither one of them is mine, but I've got a hunch you're not gonna like it either way." Zeke was sitting behind the wheel, because he and Grady had agreed that Grady was too upset to drive, neither of them mentioning that he'd polished off Zeke's very expensive bottle of wine while he changed clothes.

"It's not my car. It's the city's."

"I'm driving a police car?" Zeke began to chuckle, and then it progressed to a full-fledged laugh. "Never thought that'd happen."

"Can't we go any faster?"

"Thompson, you're a cop. You see that wreck up there? We can't get through until they clean it up."

"Right. What about through the park?"

"Passed that turnoff a half-mile back. Any suggestions about how we get back there again?" Zeke considered the matter for a moment. "Do we have one of those red lights for the top of this thing?"

"Right here," Stacy chipped in from the back seat of the car.

"Put it back, Stacy. If we use it, we'll just get in trouble." It surprised Grady that Zeke was the one who said it. "Look, Thompson—"

"Would you call me Grady, already? I'm not arresting you, for God's sake."

"I should hope not. Okay, look, Grady, the only way you're gonna get there faster than this is to walk. It's too far to walk. That means you can just sit tight until we get there."

"But Hilary—"

"Don't worry. She's still there. Even if they could put her on the next flight, she'd never be able to sort her shoes and pack this fast."

"All her shoes are at my house."

"That settles it, then. She'll be there. Hilary goes nowhere without her shoes."

# 10

WHEN PAUL, MICHAEL and Hilary bought the firehouse three years before, one of its chief attractions had been the huge expanse of unbroken space they'd designated as the living room. They'd envisioned it as a perfect setting for parties, big enough to accommodate everyone they knew—and everyone *they* knew—with plenty of room to spare. While that assumption had always seemed as infrangible as if it were carved in stone, it had shown signs of cracking under the strain a half hour earlier. Since then, more people had arrived, shattering it beyond repair.

An uninitiated observer probably would have worried that the room itself might explode by the time the night was through. Even more than the numbers, the demographics were cause for alarm. Only the firehouse trio, with their diverse natures and respective groups of acquaintances, could have assembled such a broad spectrum of humanity in one place at one time: academics from the university and pro football players, the Fringe Element crowd and socialites, gay-rights activists and artsy types and cops. The mix was bound to produce interesting results after the various factions got into the spirit of things and quit eyeing each other as if searching for weapons; at the moment, however, it looked and felt like the prelude to a gang confrontation.

For once, Hilary wasn't worried about the potential for mayhem. As a veteran of such gatherings, she knew it was just a matter of time before the barriers were breached and the party would begin to sustain itself without intervention from the three of them. She just wished it would happen soon, so she could quietly disappear. It wasn't easy trying to maintain a facade of normalcy when what she really wanted to do was go upstairs, pull the covers over her head and howl. If she did that, however, everyone there would know that her latest victim, like the others, had decided she was more than a sane man could endure.

It was bad enough knowing that some people there already had a pretty good idea what had happened, she noted disconsolately as yet another whispered discussion came to a complete and immediate halt as she approached. She guessed Grady's conspicuous absence told them everything they wanted to know. She probably should have been disturbed by the ensuing silence—or embarrassed, as *they* were. Instead, she felt absurdly grateful that no one said anything that conveyed either ridicule or pity. It was hard for her to say which of the two had been worse in the past. This time, it didn't matter either way, because the end result was the same—Grady was lost to her forever.

That thought sent a surge of despair rushing through her, threatening her hard-won control, and Hilary knew she had to get out immediately, before she broke down and sobbed like a baby. A quick glance at her first choice of flight, the spiral staircase up to her room, eliminated that alternative—there were so many people on the steps, it was blocked as far up as she could see. She knew the hallway to the main entrance was equally congested, with overflow as well as new arrivals, and she couldn't imagine where they were all going to stand if they ever actually got into the living room.

An abortive effort to breathe validated Hilary's suspicion that air was becoming a scarce commodity, possibly even an endangered one. Her chest tightened alarmingly and she felt cold sweat trickle down her spine as she realized she was trapped, with no way out of the throng. Her heart began to pound and she chewed on her bottom lip while she searched frantically for an escape route that didn't seem to exist.

Just as a full-blown panic attack looked like a distinct—and mortifying—possibility, she spied Paul across the room, on his way into the kitchen. Letting out the air she'd been saving in her lungs, just in case, she shoved her way through the crowd and followed after him.

GRADY HADN'T EXPECTED to be greeted with open arms on his arrival at the firehouse, but he *had* expected to be noticed. No one, however, gave him a second glance, except for the very large, very scary-looking man he shouldered aside in an effort to get from the hall into the living room.

It was a wasted effort. Once he got in, there was no place to go from there. Behind him, Zeke and Stacy were wedged in the doorway, unable to move either forward or back in the crush. Stunned by both the number and density of the guests, he craned his neck as he looked for a vacant patch of floor. As far as he could tell, there weren't any to be found.

An endless sea of humans loomed before him and he idly wondered exactly how many sections of the fire code were being violated here. He hadn't known that anybody knew this many people. *He* certainly didn't; and he was relatively certain he didn't know anyone here at all. He didn't see Hilary, Paul or Michael anywhere and he swiveled his head, looking for the hosts of the melee. Any one

of them would have done at the moment, as long as he
could find a familiar face.

As he searched, the mass of bodies began to resolve itself into individuals and, to his relief, he actually recognized some of them. It wasn't quite the definitive
reassurance he had hoped for, however, since it seemed as
if everyone he knew was somewhere far across the room.
The barrier of the crowd was so absolute, they might as
well have been on the moon for all the good it did him to
have found them.

A tap on his shoulder reminded him that Zeke and Stacy
were still trapped in the doorway behind him. He turned
his head to tell them he didn't believe forward movement
was feasible and he heard Zeke hiss, "See anyone you
know?"

Grady nodded his head and pointed out Charlie and
Jenny, frowning as he did—it didn't do a lot of good to
identify people when it would take a sky hook to get to
them. Before he could verbalize that observation, Zeke
nudged him aside and plunged headlong into the mass,
towing Stacy along by one elbow. Recognizing compe-
tence when he saw it, Grady followed Zeke as he cut a path
across the room, filling in the gaps he and Stacy left before they could be reclaimed.

Because simultaneously keeping pace with Zeke and
scanning the crowd for any sign of Hilary commanded the
bulk of Grady's attention, they had almost arrived when
he noticed the young man standing beside Charlie and
Jenny, talking to them as if they'd known each other forever. Since Charlie and Jenny hadn't been along on the
dead-of-night trip to Wheeling to bail Manny Cassimatis
out of jail, Grady could only assume they'd all been

trapped in the same corner long enough for a rapport to have developed among them.

Zeke and Manny greeted one another like the old friends they were and then Zeke introduced the younger man to Stacy, who looked as if she thought Manny was even cuter than Brandon Pengelly. Grady was still dealing with the sudden urge he had to let Manny know Stacy was only fifteen, when Manny turned to Grady and said, "Why, if it isn't Grady Thompson, Ree's—"

"I am not," Grady interrupted tersely, "a pervert. Nor am I a victim."

Charlie and Zeke both began to laugh; Jenny and Stacy just looked confused.

"I didn't say either one," Manny defended himself.

"You were going to," Grady accused.

"C'mon, Stacy," Zeke interceded quickly. "Let's get something to drink."

As Zeke towed her back into the mob, Grady called after them, "Only pop. You hear me, Zeke?"

"Got it!" the deep voice returned, its source already out of sight.

"I'll make sure," Jenny offered, following after them.

Grady turned back to the two men. "So where is she? She hasn't left yet, has she?"

"Left?" they both echoed.

"For France," Grady prompted.

Manny and Charlie threw back their heads and laughed heartily, further inflaming Grady.

"Dammit . . ."

Although Charlie was still incapable of speech, Manny forcibly reined in his laughter to a mere chuckle. "Paul called you?"

Grady stared at him for a moment before he realized
Hilary's housemate had successfully manipulated him yet
again. When the revelation occurred, his face went white,
then red, then white again before he choked out, "She's
here?"

"Tickets for France aren't until January, after the end of
the term," Charlie volunteered.

"Why," Grady demanded through gritted teeth, "did he
do this to me?"

Manny and Charlie just grinned.

"Where is she?"

"Kitchen, I think."

This time, Grady didn't need Zeke's intercession to get
across the room. The grim expression on his face cleared
the way for him.

But when he plowed through the swing door into the
kitchen, only Paul was there. Completely unastonished
by Grady's appearance, he looked up at him and remarked, "It's about time you got here."

Grady's irritation evaporated in the face of Paul's can-
dor. How could he be angry with someone who manipulated him and then candidly admitted it, especially when
it was only in the service of a good cause? "Hilary?" he
asked.

Paul grinned triumphantly and cocked his head in the
direction of the pantry. "In there. She's looking for more
napkins."

Grady gave Paul a pleading look, which earned him
another radiant grin. "If you happen to run across any, just
pitch them out the door."

As Paul pushed open the kitchen door to return to the
party, he turned and added, "Can I be maid of honor?"

Grady gaped at him for an instant and then he, too, began to laugh. "That's one you and Hilary are going to have to work out between yourselves. I'm not going near it."

After Paul's departure, Grady inhaled deeply in an effort to compose himself, walked into the pantry and pulled the door shut behind him.

Hilary was so preoccupied by her search for the napkins, she didn't hear Grady enter the room or close the door. Oblivious to his presence, she continued to dig through the shelves lining the small, windowless room. Grady decided to take advantage of the opportunity to observe Hilary discreetly.

Before she'd fled his house that afternoon, he'd been too agitated to notice her appearance. He regretted it now, because she really looked lovely. The gleaming satin clung to her upper torso, accentuating the dainty narrowness of her waist. The billowing skirt and sleeves merely heightened the effect. It all shimmered in the dim light provided by the single fixture in the ceiling, as did her tumble of curls. Each time she moved, the sight reminded Grady of bright flame.

That was Hilary, Grady thought. An alluring flame he couldn't resist, in spite of the consequences. Every time he saw her, he was overwhelmed by the desire to immerse himself in her until she consumed him. If this was insanity, he didn't care.

He sighed and Hilary heard it, whirling around to face him with a flash of light and a rustle of satin. For a moment, she stood and stared at him, pale, wide-eyed and speechless in his unexpected presence.

Because his face was shadowed, Hilary couldn't see his expression and wasn't reassured by his arrival. It was entirely possible he was only there because he wasn't fin-

ished yelling at her yet. She didn't like the idea much, but
she didn't see any way around it. He was, after all, entitled to be furious, after everything he had endured.

It was the first time she had ever seen Grady in a suit.
His chest and shoulders looked even broader than she
knew they were, and the jacket tapered to his slim waist
and hips. Her gaze followed the muscles of his thighs
downward to the reflected glimmer of the shiny black
shoes on his feet. When she glanced back up she saw the
new tie. The observation gave her hope—not that Grady
wanted her back, but that he intended to part with her on
friendly terms, at least.

"Grady, I'm sorry," Hilary ventured. "I shouldn't
have—"

"Hilary, why did you run?"

She stopped, stunned. After a moment's silence, she
squeaked, "Excuse me?"

"I asked why you ran," he repeated, stepping into the
light.

She saw that he didn't look angry, and it puzzled her.
Although she opened her mouth and then closed it again
several times, no words emerged.

"You thought I was going to end it, didn't you?" he demanded. "You really thought I was going to tell you to
pack your things and go?"

She nodded. "I . . ."

He sighed again. "Haven't you figured out by now that
I'm not going to do that?"

"I tried so hard, Grady!" she finally burst out. "But,
even then, I could see it wasn't going to work! I can't do
it! You see that now, don't you?"

"Hilary, I love you. You love me, don't you?"

She nodded, and tears welled up in her eyes.

"I love you for what you are, Hilary, and part of that is this—" he flailed for the word for a moment "—chaos. You wouldn't be you without it."

Her anguish turned to puzzlement and she began to wring her hands together against her skirt.

"Call it a character flaw, Hilary, but I love the chaos, too." He chuckled to himself and she was forced to join him. "Do you remember, the first time we met, I called you 'an attractive nuisance'?"

She nodded and smiled tremulously.

"Maybe that's what you are, but you're *my* attractive nuisance." He jabbed his finger against his chest possessively. "I don't want calm with someone else, and I can't stand the idea of you creating chaos in some other man's life."

"And if I make you crazy?"

"I'm getting used to it."

"And when things happen?" she prompted, a touch of apprehension remaining in her voice.

He shrugged. "They happen. I yell. You yell back." He grinned at her meaningfully. "And then we have a hell of a good time making up."

Hilary finally returned his smile without hesitation.

"If you come here, I'll show you how that part works." Grady reached out with one hand and she stepped toward him.

Hilary moved into his arms and it was like coming home after a long exile, though they'd made love only the night before. Grady's explosion that afternoon had left her with the conviction that their relationship was finished, and she'd already resigned herself to the fact that she would never again be held or kissed or caressed by him. It was an immense relief to have herself proved wrong.

Their embrace was natural and instinctive and their bodies fit together like two halves of a single unit. Her arms slipped up behind his neck, and his, around her waist. Her head rose as his bent down to hers and their mouths melded together intimately, his tongue finding shelter in her sweetness. Her breasts nestled against his chest and he felt her swollen nipples jut into his ribs through the heavy fabric of her dress. Despite the fluffy crinolines of her skirt, she felt his hard masculine strength cupped against the soft heart of her femininity.

When Grady's mouth finally left Hilary's, it was only to move to the most sensitive spot at the side of her throat, just under her ear. As he nipped at it with his teeth and then soothed it with his tongue, her head tilted back to allow him greater access and she emitted a weak, keening sound that made him want to roar with triumph.

Her knees going limp, she sagged against him, and he backed up until he reached a stepstool that was pushed against the end wall. Sitting on it to stabilize himself, he pulled her between his legs and continued his loving assault. His hand closed over her breast, generating warm ripples of pleasure that radiated through her body as she pressed herself more snugly into his palm.

Through the haze of her own desire, Hilary recognized the extent of Grady's passion when her hand brushed against him. His hard length indicated that he was unmistakably aroused and she smiled, gratified to know she had the same uncontrollable effect on him that he had on her. Acting of its own will, since she had none of her own, her hand turned and her fingers closed over him through the fabric of his trousers.

With a shuddering groan, Grady lowered his head to her upper chest, exposed above the square neckline of her dress. His lips traced the ridge of her collarbone with tender thoroughness before moving lower to the topmost curves of her breasts. He nuzzled against her until his exploration was obstructed by the edge of her dress. Feeling the hard nipple beneath his hand and the slippery satin, he wanted it in his mouth.

Hilary, too, hungered for more intimate contact. A liquid heat built inside her as she felt her body begin to prepare itself for him. She was totally mindless of everything but the incredible yearning he created within her and the powerful reactions he exhibited to her caresses. Where they were, the party out in the firehouse, the possibility of discovery—all became meaningless as she eased down the zipper of his fly and slipped her hand inside.

When Hilary touched him, the last vestiges of Grady's awareness of time and place vanished completely as his senses overwhelmed the thinking part of his brain. The entire world was reduced to the hard part of him that ached for her intimate softness and sensitivity. He tugged at the upper edge of her dress in an effort to bare her breasts, but the bodice was too snug. Sliding his other hand up from the small of her back, he searched for the zipper.

Still fumbling for it moments later, Grady made a noise of frustration. Apparently misinterpreting it, she tightened her hand and he was forced to grab her wrist to stop her before she incited him beyond control.

"No," Grady choked out painfully. "Don't do that or I'll . . . Where's the zipper in this thing?"

"Oh." Hilary raised her left arm. "It's in the side."

"Thank you." He kissed her firmly before locating the little tab under her arm and lowering it past her waist.

The mere act of unzipping her dress was an erotic experience for Hilary. At the sudden loosening of her bodice, her breasts dropped, and her already-sensitized nipples brushed against the fabric. Emitting a soft, whimpering cry, she leaned toward Grady, capturing his mouth for another, deeper kiss.

His hand slipped inside her dress and each of them enjoyed the erotic illusion of nakedness while remaining fully clothed. They kissed and caressed until both were pushed almost beyond their limits.

Balanced on one of Grady's thighs, Hilary shifted restlessly, desperate for release. Grady, noting her need, thrust his hand under the bulk of the skirt and crinolines and finally found her. She was warm and wet and so ready, the heady scent of it made him wild. "Please, Hilary...."

She gaped at him, and whispered, "Here?"

"Here," he affirmed before he kissed her again and moved his fingers in a manner that would have made her say yes to anything, anywhere. "Please say yes—now—I need—" he gasped.

"But, how...?" she began, glancing skeptically at the floor behind her.

Wordlessly, Grady removed Hilary from his thigh and rose from the stepstool. His pants and shorts, already loosened and shoved down, fell to puddle around his feet. After toeing off his shoes, he retrieved his clothing and tossed it onto one of the shelves. He knelt before her and peeled off her panty hose, kissing the juncture between her legs as he did. Sitting on the stool again, he pulled her back onto his lap.

Her dress crushed between their bodies, she straddled him and he guided himself into her waiting warmth. As he entered her, he groaned and she emitted a wordless cry that communicated both relief and surrender. Sliding his hands to her hips, he clutched them and arched himself upward. With his assistance, she began to move over him, at first slowly and then with a steadily escalating rhythm. The pressure already created in each of them quickly blossomed and burst gloriously in a flood of ecstasy more spectacular than either of them could have imagined.

Afterward, Hilary slumped against Grady's chest, spent and exhausted. When she could finally speak, she murmured, "If making up is always like this, I'd better start thinking of things to do to make you mad."

Grady chuckled and pressed a tender kiss to the damp ringlets at her temple. "I doubt that's going to be a problem."

She raised her head from his shoulder and looked into his eyes. "Grady, I really don't try. These things—"

"Just happen," he finished for her. "I know that, sweetheart."

"Speaking of which, have you any ideas as to how we're going to get out of here gracefully?"

"Not yet, but when I think of one, I'll let you know." He stroked her back soothingly and suddenly stopped. "You weren't wearing underwear, were you?"

Hilary giggled. "The way it's made, I can't—"

"Never mind." He put his fingers to her lips to stop her explanation and she nipped at one playfully. "If I'd known you weren't wearing any, I'd have jumped on you immediately."

"Instead of waiting thirty seconds?" she teased. "Stacy asked if she could borrow it."

"Stacy, in a dress without underwear? Not a chance. I'm sending her to a convent tomorrow, and they can keep her until she's twenty-one." They both laughed for a moment, imagining Stacy's reaction to such a suggestion.

Grady's laughter stopped first. A heartbeat later, he said without warning, "Let's get married, Hilary. Tonight."

Hilary's breath caught in her throat, and she gaped at him speechlessly.

"Hilary, you know I want to marry you and spend the rest of our lives together," he said, sounding more reasonable than she thought he should, considering that his sanity had taken off for parts unknown. "Let's do it."

"Tonight?" she finally squeaked.

"Tonight." Although his tone was decisive as he repeated the word, there was an expression of hopeful uncertainty in his eyes that touched her deep inside. "Why wait, Hilary?"

In light of the fact that Grady had clearly abdicated his role as the sensible one, Hilary felt obligated to give the question thorough consideration.

Misinterpreting her silence, Grady hastily amended, "You've never been married before, so you want a real wedding, with a dress and your parents and everything, don't you? If that's it, I'll wait."

She shook her head and laughed softly. "It's not that. I've planned enough weddings—for myself and other people—that it really doesn't bother me if I don't have to do it again. And I know my folks don't want to hear the word *wedding* again in connection with me unless it's already an accomplished fact."

"Then, what is it?"

"There's a three-day waiting period before we can get a marriage license," she explained patiently. "And, it's a weekend, so none of the offices are open, anyway."

Grady simply smiled, as if he knew something she didn't.

"You want to help me out here? Being practical isn't what I do best. I don't get a lot of practice."

"Maryland," he said firmly.

"Excuse me?"

"There *is* no waiting period in Maryland, and it's only a couple of hours away," he pointed out. "We can be down there and married by midnight."

Grady watched as Hilary's expression slowly changed, from dumbstruck to realization to beaming happiness. As the transformation occurred, he tightened his arms around her waist and a great weight lifted from his chest, freeing him to breathe.

"Maryland!" She kissed him soundly. "That's it, Grady! You're a genius!"

He basked in her praise for a moment before he asked, "Now that I've solved that problem, do you think you could provide a solution for how we're going to get out of here?"

Her blue eyes wide with horror, she clapped one hand over her mouth and muttered through it, "Oh, Lord, all those people out there...."

He nodded in silent agreement.

Hilary clambered off Grady's lap and retrieved their clothing. When she turned back to give Grady his pants, he was still sitting on the stool. From the torso up, he was fully dressed—his suit jacket, shirt and tie all in place, if a bit rumpled. Below that, however, his shirttails hung askew and a long expanse of bare leg extended down to his matching socks. The sight was endearing and funny and sexy, all at the same time, and she couldn't quite decide whether she wanted to pat him on the head, laugh or climb back onto his lap. Sternly she reminded herself that she would have a lifetime to look at Grady half-dressed and then handed him his pants.

Despite a few distractions, they managed to restore their hair and clothing to some semblance of order. Grady went to the door to do a bit of prudent reconnaissance. After inching it open, he listened for signs of activity in the kitchen. Hearing none, he opened the door wide and they emerged from the pantry with profound mutual sighs of relief.

Their entry into the living room revealed why their privacy in the pantry had not been violated: Paul and Ryan were standing guard outside the kitchen door, ready to challenge anyone who wanted to go into the kitchen. What their action lacked in discretion, it made up for in results.

Paul looked at them expectantly. "Well?"

Hilary and Grady both smiled at him silently, neither of them willing to give him the satisfaction of an answer before he begged for it.

"When's the wedding?" he demanded, his voice filled with irritation.

Hilary gave him another moment to stew before she answered his question. "Tonight. We're going to Maryland."

Paul whooped, drawing the attention of the guests in the immediate vicinity.

"Hilary's agreed to get married, and we're going to Maryland tonight," Grady announced proudly.

"I can get a couple of limos with one call," offered Zeke, who was standing nearby. After Hilary's acceptance, he shoved through the crowd to use the telephone in the kitchen.

The news traveled rapidly across the room, until all the guests knew their plan. Toasts were proposed and congratulations given, until Hilary and Grady were both overwhelmed by the expressions of good cheer. Even the sight of the seven ex-fiancés shaking their heads in collective, stunned amazement couldn't daunt their high spirits.

At last, Charlie emerged from the mob, towing Jenny behind him with one hand and Stacy with the other. Stacy immediately broke free from his grasp and threw her arms around Hilary's neck with an excited squeal. "You're going to marry Daddy!"

Over Stacy's shoulder, Hilary's gaze met Grady's and both of them winced at the piercing sound.

Stacy gave Hilary a final squeeze that threatened her ribs, then turned, launched herself at Grady and began the performance all over again. It was finally brought to a halt by Zeke's return from the kitchen with the news that the limousines would be at the firehouse within the hour.

While Zeke and Grady sorted out the transportation arrangements, Hilary, Stacy and Jenny all went upstairs to Hilary's bedroom on the third floor to make repairs to Hilary's hair and makeup. Stacy offered to lend her locket for "something borrowed," which Hilary gratefully accepted, along with Jenny's help in touching up her hair with the curling iron. She refused to acknowledge Jenny's speculative glance as she dug through the drawer in search of fresh panties and hose. Finally she grabbed them and stalked into the bathroom, away from the other woman.

Once she was alone, the first twinges of panic threatened her sense of equilibrium. Her familiarity with the sensation allowed her to recognize it immediately and there was a brief internal struggle while she reminded her-

self that she had already agreed to marry Grady, the man
she loved and who loved her enough to live in the constant shadow of disaster. For the second time that evening, she resorted to Michael's meditation exercises, this
time with greater success, because she was able to use the
image of Grady's face as a focus this time. When she regained her composure and her breathing returned to normal, she tugged on the panties and hose and went back
into the bedroom to allow Jenny and Stacy to finish
combing out her hair.

"The limos are here!" Paul's excited yell carried up to
them from the bottom of the spiral staircase.

Although a fresh surge of panic welled up in Hilary, she
took a deep breath and vanquished it before going down
the stairs to where Grady waited for her. To her astonishment, everyone who'd been in the living room when she
went upstairs was gone. Somehow the men had effected a
hasty conclusion to the party during her absence. The few
people remaining—herself and Grady, Charlie and Jenny,
Stacy, Paul, Ryan, Michael and Zeke—piled into the cars
Zeke had commandeered from some unknown source.

As she slid into the limousine, Hilary narrowly missed
crushing a box on the back seat. "Zeke!" she called out as
she put the box on her lap. "Somebody left something in
here. What should I do . . . ?"

"Open it!" he yelled back as he got into the other car.

She did. Inside was a small bouquet of carnations,
daisies, and roses and a rose boutonniere for Grady's la-
pel. She smiled happily. Lord only knew what favor Zeke
had called in to get them at that time on a Friday night.

Grady slipped in next to her and looked down at the
flowers. "Zeke must have made more than one call while
he was in the kitchen." He held up a bottle of champagne

Zeke had shoved into his hands just as he'd left the fire-house.

Hilary looked at the label on the bottle. "This is his private stock. Can't get this in Pennsylvania."

"It figures," Grady muttered under his breath.

WHEN THEY ARRIVED in Maryland several hours later, Hilary was the calmest bride ever seen on the face of the earth. Grady, however, was a nervous wreck.

With the serenity of a Madonna, Hilary filled out the papers for the license, because Grady's hands shook too much for him to write. The only thing he had to do was sign them, but even then, she had to remind him what his middle name was. She didn't jab him with the pin when she put on his boutonniere—a maneuver he was quite certain he could never have completed alone. Her bouquet was steady in her hands as they stood before the official for the ceremony.

As they spoke their vows, Hilary's voice was firm and clear in contrast with Grady's, which sounded every bit as nervous as he was. When they reached the point where the magistrate asked for the ring, Grady almost lost it totally as he emitted a harsh choke at the sudden, horrified realization that he didn't have one.

"That's all right," Hilary told him understandingly, patting him on the arm. "We'll get one later." She turned to the magistrate with a radiant smile. "We forgot it."

"Wait," a deep voice behind them interrupted and everyone turned to look at Zeke, who was digging in his pockets. "I've got it here somewhere."

He finally located the ring and handed it to Grady. It was an elegantly simple band. With a grateful smile to Zeke, Grady accepted it and passed it along to the magistrate.

When the ceremony was concluded and Hilary and Grady were pronounced husband and wife, everyone, including the happy couple, gave a collective sigh of relief.

"You may now kiss the bride."

Hilary turned to Grady, who had somehow, in the last few seconds, regained his normal composure. His hands were confident on her shoulders as he lowered his face to hers and kissed her twice—the first, just a skim of her lips; the second, a longer kiss that made her knees weak.

After thanking the official, they all piled back into the limousines to return to Pittsburgh. As their car pulled onto the interstate, Hilary snuggled against Grady's side and looked down at her left hand wonderingly.

Reading her accurately, Grady murmured, "So how does it feel, being a wife?"

She looked first at him and then down at the ring again. "Permanent. Secure. I like it."

With a soft laugh, he raised her hand to his lips and pressed a kiss over the ring.

Both of them were oblivious to anything but each other until Charlie's muttered curse caught their attention. As they raised their heads in response, the first thing they noticed was red-and-blue flashing lights. Before anyone could say anything more, they heard the siren and felt the limousine slow down as it slid over to stop on the shoulder of the highway.

"I—" Hilary began.

Grady interrupted the apology he knew was coming. "I love you, Hilary. I married you, remember? Now just shut up, for God's sake." And as the sirens wailed and the red and blue lights flickered over them, he prayed that the Maryland State Police had a sense of humor. He didn't want to spend his wedding night in jail.